Pat

Ecstasy Romance ®

HE CLAIMED HER WITH A KISS
THAT COULD ONLY BE DESCRIBED
AS MIND-SHATTERING . . .

Instead of offering a token resistance merely out of some
misplaced sense of pride, Sam met his assault with urgency. Her lips moved sensuously beneath his, coaxing
. . . reacquainting themselves with a part of him that had
given her such pleasure.

With a boldness born of thirsting desire, Sam knew instinctively the state of his arousal. One part of her reveled
in her ability to carry him to such a fever pitch of excitement. The other was insatiable in pursuit of her own
needs. When she felt his lips on the sensitive throbbing
pulse of her throat, she was unable to stifle the low,
purring sounds that escaped from her parted lips. . . .

A CANDLELIGHT ECSTASY ROMANCE ®

LOVING EXILE

ELEANOR WOODS

A CANDLELIGHT ECSTASY ROMANCE ®

Published by
Dell Publishing Co., Inc.
1 Dag Hammarskjold Plaza
New York, New York 10017

ISBN: 0–440–14650–X

Printed in the United States of America
First printing—May 1983

To Our Readers:

We have been delighted with your enthusiastic response to Candlelight Ecstasy Romances®, and we thank you for the interest you have shown in this exciting series.

In the upcoming months we will continue to present the distinctive sensuous love stories you have come to expect only from Ecstasy. We look forward to bringing you many more books from your favorite authors and also the very finest work from new authors of contemporary romantic fiction.

As always, we are striving to present the unique, absorbing love stories that you enjoy most—books that are more than ordinary romance.

Your suggestions and comments are always welcome. Please write to us at the address below.

Sincerely,

The Editors
Candlelight Romances
1 Dag Hammarskjold Plaza
New York, New York 10017

LOVING EXILE

CHAPTER ONE

There was an unobtrusive similarity between the two young women sitting at the small table. Not so much in looks as in spirit—kindred souls, as it were.

They were enjoying a rare lunch together at Antoine's, their favorite restaurant, with one limiting herself to an enormous salad while trying not to drool over the delicious oysters Foch her companion was having.

"How can you sit there and eat that glorious concoction while I'm forced to make do with this damned produce patch?" Claire Renaud, the elder of the two by six years, asked her sister-in-law with open disgust. She was an attractive brunette, with a sparkling wit and an engaging smile.

"That bad, huh?" Sam grinned mischievously, not

in the least repentant. "You shouldn't keep yourself on such a strict diet, Claire. You've hardly gained any weight. In fact, there are times when I'm convinced this pregnancy of yours is nothing but a myth," she teased. She leaned back in her chair, her emerald-green eyes sparkling with amusement.

Samantha Ewing, Sam to her friends and family, was a petite brunette. Her heart-shaped face and creamy complexion were pleasing to the eye. She was twenty-six years old, a warm, gentle person by nature, but she could just as easily become quite formidable if pushed too far.

"Believe me, after enduring the discomfort of morning sickness, I'm convinced. Your niece or nephew has been most uncooperative thus far," Claire ruefully remarked.

"And my dear brother? Is he showering you with sympathy and understanding, or does he sternly lecture you that your misery is all in your head?" Sam asked scornfully.

Claire chuckled. The feud between Jacques and Sam seemed never to run out of steam. "Believe it or not, he's been a perfect angel. In fact, he's really spoiling me."

"Mmmmm . . ." was Sam's only comment. Privately her thoughts were not so generous. To her way of thinking her brother was the most pompous, small-minded person she'd ever known.

The fact that Jacques had had to assume responsibility for Sam when she was only eight years old—

while he was in his early twenties—hadn't changed her opinion in the least.

Jacques Renaud! Oh, what romantic flights of fancy the name brought to mind, Samantha thought fleetingly. A swashbuckling hero, arrayed in a white shirt of finest lawn, fully gathered sleeves at shoulder and cuffs, tight-fitting knee breeches. Standing on the deck of his ship, his feet braced apart, glorying in the feel of the sun and wind caressing his bronzed features. Shaking his fist at his enemy, daring them to attack! Or perhaps a Rhett Butler, seeing Scarlett safely through a flaming Atlanta, his muscled arms and shoulders straining to their very limit as he accomplishes the harrowing task. But once the feat is accomplished, sweeping up the woman he loves in his arms and kissing her punishingly.

But, no . . . her brother was the exact opposite in character, if not in looks. He was handsome—that much she grudgingly gave him, but there was a limit to charity. To sum it, or him, up in a nutshell, Jacques was a twit, with the mind of a computer. And poor, kindhearted Claire would be forced to spend the rest of her life with that humorless prig. Worst of all, the most intimate side of their marriage could be nothing short of a nightmare—or so Samantha surmised. She couldn't imagine Jacques as being anything but a cold fish.

"How's Elizabeth?" Claire asked, choosing a subject she knew would divert Sam's attention from Jacques.

13

"As mischievous as ever. She's beginning to climb. I honestly believe she's part mountain goat."

Her thirteen-month-old daughter was the joy of her life. Unfortunately John Ewing, Sam's husband, had died before his daughter's birth.

Sam had had to endure the months of her pregnancy alone, and at times the realization that she was solely responsible for raising her child frightened her out of her wits. But she'd gotten through it, and Claire . . . as well as Jacques, had been with her during the cesarean birth. Sam would never forget her sister-in-law's support. As for her brother, she could just as easily have done without his presence. His overanxious hovering—a side of him Sam had never seen before—had almost driven her crazy.

"Can you and Elizabeth have dinner with us later in the week?" Claire broke into Sam's thoughts.

"What?" Sam asked, somewhat confused, then smiled. "You'd better let me call you. I'm absolutely swamped with work at the moment."

"Try to make it if you can, and don't forget to . . ." Claire's voice trailed off, her attention distracted by the arrival of a large party. Bringing up the rear of the group was Greg Howland, listening with obvious concentration to the man beside him, who was none other than her husband, Jacques.

"Er . . . Sam . . . honey, I think we should go now. There's a sale going on at Marie's. I'd really like to see what they've got." Claire turned in her chair and tried to catch their waiter's eye.

"I'm sorry, love, but I'm afraid I can't go with you. I have an appointment in thirty minutes."

"Oh . . ." Claire replied inanely, watching with something akin to horror as the maître d' began walking forward, his eyes on a large table directly behind them.

"Samantha, do not—under any circumstances— look around. Understand?" At Sam's surprised nod Claire went on, leaning as far across the table as was possible. "Greg and Jacques, along with several other men, are headed this way. To the table behind us, I presume."

"Greg? Greg who?" Sam asked, feeling a shaft of fear surge through her at the mention of the name. With a calmness she had never dreamed herself capable of she reached for her wineglass and raised it to her lips.

"Greg Howland! Your former husband. The man you were married to for a year, for God's sake?" Claire hurriedly exclaimed, amazed by Sam's indifferent response to her announcement.

Sam carefully set her glass down, then touched the large linen napkin to her lips. Her only outward reaction was the sudden pallor of her face. "You mustn't get so upset, Claire. The baby has enough going against it with Jacques for a father," she calmly replied.

"Did you hear what I said, Sam? It's Greg," Claire hissed in an urgent undertone.

"Oh . . . I heard all right. But short of hiding under

the table or tearing off to the ladies' room, what do you expect me to do?"

"I'm . . . I'm not sure," Claire murmured weakly, her fingers tightly gripping the edge of the table.

By then the party was upon them, and Jacques could see his wife and sister. It occurred to Claire, in the brief moment when their eyes met, that he seemed to be caught in the throes of some horrible affliction!

Before Jacques could move, one of the men in the party noticed the two women and hurried toward them, an engaging grin on his face.

"Sam! You little devil. I can't believe it's really you." He engulfed her hand in his giant paw, squeezing it, then kissed her warmly on the cheek.

"Hello, Sean." Her dark green eyes warmed to a younger version of Greg. For a moment her heart almost stopped beating as the pain tore at her, leaving her emotions naked and vulnerable.

As she stared up into Sean's face Sam was dimly aware of her brother bending to kiss Claire, his murmured words of greeting—of the other members of the party taking their seats at the adjoining table, all but one. Greg had remained standing next to Jacques, his gaze riveted on Sam.

Sean's handsome face glowed with genuine affection. "Well, Sam, I'd heard you were back. Is it temporary or permanent?"

"Oh, it's definitely permanent." She smiled, feeling the muscles in her face trembling, exactly as if she had just suffered a severe shock. She then let her eyes linger on Jacques, who was staring at her with a stricken expression on his face.

"Hello, Jacques."

"Samantha . . ." His curt nod left no doubt of his disapproval at finding her enjoying a leisurely lunch while he was forced to hover embarrassed in the background. "I wasn't aware you and Claire had made plans for lunch," he added, accusingly.

"Was there some reason we shouldn't have?" she asked innocently.

"Of course not," he said stiffly. "I was merely curious, that's all." He patted Claire's shoulder absentmindedly, and then walked the few steps to the adjoining table.

Now that this first meeting with Greg was upon her, Sam knew she must find the courage to see it through. It took every ounce of willpower she possessed to raise her green-eyed gaze and meet the smoldering depths of his own piercing stare.

The initial point of contact was devastating to Sam. It was all she could do to steel her features into a smiling mask of friendliness . . . in light of the contempt emanating from Greg.

Her only moment of victory, if indeed there was one, was knowing he was forced to acknowledge her presence . . . a problem that seemed to be causing him considerable difficulty.

His dark green eyes were almost literally darting jets of fire; the heavy brows added a sinister look to

17

his rugged features. There was a slightly grayish tinge in the area of his nostrils and lips, leaving Sam . . . as well as Sean and Claire, in no doubt as to his frame of mind.

"How . . . how are you, Greg?" Sam finally broke the explosive silence.

"I'm fine, Samantha." His deep voice rushed over her like warm spring water on a hot summer's day. "And you?"

"Quite well, thank you," Sam huskily replied. At that precise moment she knew she'd endured all she could of his contemptuous scrutiny. She turned back to Claire, her appetite having suddenly vanished. "Thank you for lunch, love. I'll give you a call later in the week." She came to her feet, flashing Sean a warm smile. "It was nice seeing you, Sean."

The same fixed smile remained glued to her face as she included Greg in her farewells, then turned and walked with unconscious grace through the crowded room and out the door.

Once outside the restaurant, Sam hurried toward the parking lot two blocks away, her spine rigid as she fought to control the horrible trembling that was racking her body.

With hands that were noticeably shaky, she unlocked the car and got in. Instead of removing the keys from her purse and starting the engine, however, Sam slumped wearily against the seat, her eyes closed.

Seeing Greg, hearing his voice . . . had proved to

be more traumatic than she'd ever imagined. But the alternative didn't bear thinking about.

For a brief moment Sam's mind and thoughts were numbed . . . totally without direction. It was only by taking deep breaths and willing herself back into a state of awareness that she was able to still the traitorous pounding of her heart.

Oh, God! she frantically thought. I simply hadn't planned on my first meeting with Greg to occur in a public place with our every move, our every gesture watched by a crowd. She had planned on seeing him though. . . . Once, shortly after moving back to New Orleans, she'd even gone so far as to telephone his office, only to be told he was out of the country; his secretary was uncertain when he would return.

Sam had considered asking Jacques for more information about Greg's whereabouts, then immediately abandoned that idea. Drawing her brother into her private life was the last thing Sam wanted, not to mention letting him guess the motive behind her curious questions.

And Jacques would be inordinately curious, Sam was sure of that. Even though they were no longer related by marriage, he and Greg had remained friends, and were quite often thrown together socially. No, she'd reasoned, swallowing her pride and trying to see Greg was one thing. Allowing her brother to gloat was unthinkable.

But now, hopefully, she wouldn't be forced to seek Greg out. For unless he'd changed . . . and drastically so . . . Sam knew he'd take the bait. He wasn't the sort of man to leave loose ends lying about. It gave Sam a tiny measure of hope that in an attempt to assuage his curiosity about her he'd find a way to see her.

"And that, my dear, brings us to the next question," she muttered in an undertone as she reached with one hand in her purse for her keys. "Are you ready for a head to head confrontation with Greg Howland? You know it won't be pleasant."

But even before the words were voiced, Sam knew the answer. Not only did she want such a meeting to occur, she was almost desperate for it. Her entire future, the driving force behind her every move in the past year, perhaps longer, had been dominated by one thing—her desire to confront Greg and to convince him that she was not the two-timing hussy he believed her to be.

Some fifteen minutes later Sam parked her light blue Volvo in the driveway of a gracious home in the Garden district of the city. There was a quiet air of dignity, a commanding presence about her, as she walked toward the front door, not a hair out of place, her features calm and serene.

The next hour was spent listening to the prospective client's ideas about what she would like to have done to the large family room, with Sam taking down the ideas in a small black notebook and adding her own suggestions.

By the time the session was over, Sam had gained

a new client for the small, exclusive firm she was associated with, and Mrs. Anders was more than pleased with her choice of decorators.

As she left the Anders home Sam was tempted to turn her car toward the interstate and drive till she was exhausted. But it was an urge that was born of desperation and fear, certainly not one to be given in to.

Sam wasn't a quitter. In the last three years of her life she'd had more than her share of grief, emotional setbacks. Losing Greg had devastated her—the subsequent divorce had cast her adrift with no purpose, no direction to her life. But that innate quest for survival that takes over in times of crisis forced her to eat, occasionally to sleep, even to manage a smile to thaw her frozen features as she'd stumbled through the first months of the process of rebuilding her shattered life.

Having seen Greg, heard the deep timbre of his voice, remembered the touch of his hands on her body, had only served to intensify the old hurts, old wounds, that had repeatedly tortured her over the past three years.

And yet there was a certain anger in her at the way he'd stood so disapprovingly before her, his face a mask of glacial hardness. To Sam, it seemed as though he was silently taunting her, daring her to face his compelling gaze, then freezing her with an icy blast of indifference.

She knew his rude behavior hadn't gone unnoticed

by Sean and Claire, and it would have been quite simple to have reacted in kind. In fact, there had been a period in her life when she would have done just that. Humiliate Greg . . . cause him the same pain and heartache he had once caused her. He had actually accused her of having an affair with Claude Favret, her employer, and refused to listen to a single word she'd offered in her own defense, which had indeed left Sam with a desire to strike back.

Then somehow the healing process began, with time and circumstances dulling the edges of her pain. . . . But included in that lengthy process had been the gradual realization that running away as she'd done had only contributed to the general impression that she was actually guilty.

The blast of the horn from the car behind her caused Sam to jump, a look of chagrin on her face, as she saw cars in the lanes on either side of her moving forward at a brisk pace. She joined the traffic, unable to control the twitching of her lips at the irate gentleman behind her, his scowling face clearly visible in her rearview mirror.

There was a determined thrust to Sam's chin as she turned off Metairie Road and into the narrow drive beside the attractive building that housed Favret Interiors, and drove around to the rear where there was ample staff parking.

Round one with Greg had been shattering . . . almost more than she could bear. There was a strange mixture of fear and anticipation as she wondered when the next skirmish would occur. And it would soon enough . . . Greg would see that it did.

Once in her office, Sam forced all other thoughts but those of her newest client from her mind and set to work drawing up the particulars to present to Claude.

With painstaking precision she drew to scale the dimensions of the room, indicating doors and windows in their proper positions. Next, she suggested fabrics to be used in recovering various pieces that were to be kept, three different window treatments she thought would enhance the overall charm of the room, wall-covering samples, along with several suggestions for the floor, including carpet or wide planking stained a dark oak color.

Finally satisfied that she'd covered every aspect of the account, Sam left her office and went in search of Claude. She found him in the large workroom in the rear of the shop, hovering over a seamstress who was working on some draperies for an account Claude was personally handling.

"Do you have time to take a look at this?" Sam asked, indicating the manila folder she held in one hand.

"Of course," Claude smiled. "Let's go into my office," he suggested, casting another anxious glance at the beautiful rust-colored velvet material.

The seamstress shot Sam a look of gratitude for

removing her nervous employer from her presence.

"I'm sure Mrs. Blane is perfectly capable of finishing these draperies without you hovering over her shoulder," Sam told him, casting a conspiratorial grin toward the older woman. "Who are those for?" she asked as they walked across to the side door of his office.

"The Longino House. Have you forgotten? We're doing the front parlor. Each participating firm has one room to decorate," Claude explained.

"Oh, yes. Now I remember. Have they definitely decided to add it to the historical register?"

"Yes. It was confirmed last week. Mrs. Grammier called me with the news."

"Are you going to donate the materials you use?" Sam asked curiously, well aware of the amount of money he'd spent, as well as time.

"Certainly. It's fantastic advertising for the firm," Claude replied.

She couldn't help smiling. Claude's munificence wasn't as unselfish as he'd like it to appear. However, in this case others would benefit from his charitable gesture as well.

In his office Claude sat at his desk and opened the folder. He looked over Sam's proposal, asking a question or two, offering a suggestion here and there. After listening to her explanations and assuring himself that all was in order, he closed the file and handed it back to her.

"Sounds fine to me, as I'm sure you knew it would."

"Well . . . I'd hoped it would pass inspection." Sam grinned. "It makes working for you a great deal easier."

Claude leaned back in his chair, a thoughtful expression on his face as he unconsciously stroked his pencil-slim mustache with one forefinger.

He could never be described as a handsome man, Sam decided as she waited for him to speak, knowing the signs well—the meditative mood as he mentally posed his questions. His features bordered on the effeminate, or so it seemed to her. Not that he was unattractive . . . far from it. It was just that his thin aristocratic features did little to excite her, plus the fact that he was a dear friend.

"Are you happy being back in New Orleans, Sam?" he surprised her by asking.

"I . . . I think so," she replied, wondering what on earth had prompted the question. "I have a job I enjoy, Elizabeth, my home. What more could one ask for?"

"How about a father for Elizabeth?"

"Why, Claude!" she exclaimed facetiously. "Are you proposing?"

"Heavens, no," he chuckled.

"Then stop meddling," Sam tartly replied. "I'm quite content with my life as it is. Marriage doesn't seem to be my forte."

Claude shrugged. "I suppose you know best. It

25

just seems a shame for Elizabeth to grow up without a father to look up to."

"Have you by any chance been talking to Jacques? I get the same lecture from him all the time. A person would think my daughter has never seen a man from the way you two go on," she said sourly.

"I'm sorry, Sam. But I've always felt partially responsible for the break between you and Greg. Even after I went to him and explained why you spent that night in my apartment, I've often wondered if he really believed me."

Sam stared at Claude, shock etched into the delicate planes of her face. "When did you talk with Greg?"

"Several weeks after you'd flown to Reno for the divorce." He grimaced. "In light of the ridiculous story you told me of how he was convinced we were having an affair, I felt it my duty to try and reason with him. Unfortunately Monica had done an excellent job of brainwashing him."

Sam stared incredulously. "Monica Woods? His secretary?"

"The same. Didn't you know that she was the one who went to Greg with that awful tale?"

"No," she whispered faintly. "He would never divulge his source. Of course I wondered often enough who could have done such a despicable thing, but it all happened so fast, so unexpectedly, I . . ." She held up her hands, completely stunned by what he'd told her. "How . . . how did you find out?"

"I happened to arrive at my apartment building one evening just as Monica did. As it turned out, she was close friends with the couple across the hall from me and was on her way to have dinner with them. Your divorce had become final that week, and naturally she was agog with curiosity. I invited her in for a drink, which she readily accepted, and proceeded to pump her.

"In her silly eagerness to impress me with the closeness of her relationship with Greg, not to mention her total loyalty, she let slip that she'd informed him of your frequent visits to my apartment. Having known her for most of her life, I didn't find it difficult to imagine her regaling your husband with her vicious story. The Monicas of this world thrive on destroying other people's lives."

"Why are you telling me this now, Claude?" Sam asked huskily.

He leaned forward, his elbows resting on the surface of the desk, his expression inscrutable. "I'm not sure. But now that you're back in the city, you're bound to run into Greg from time to time. There's even the possibility that you'll be thrown together socially. I feel that you should be aware of the deep hostility, the deep-seated anger he feels toward you."

"What was Greg's reaction to your . . . er . . . confession?" she asked, unable to curb the tremor in her voice as she listened to the unbelievable story.

Claude smiled, albeit halfheartedly. "Anger, rage.

27

For one incredible moment I thought he was going to rearrange my face. I tell you, Samantha, it was most disconcerting," he admitted, running one slim hand over his immaculately groomed hair.

"I'm sorry, Claude. Greg can be quite intimidating," she said, mentally blanching at the thought of him accosting poor Claude.

CHAPTER TWO

Claude's incredible story stayed with Sam as she drove home through the late afternoon traffic. She chided herself for even caring that Greg considered her an unfaithful hussy, but deep down in her heart she knew she did care.

She'd never forgotten the contemptuous curl of his lips, the disgust stamped on the granite hardness of his face as he'd lashed out at her.

"Claude Favret!" he'd thundered in a towering rage. "You dare stand there and deny that you're sleeping with him, when I have witnesses to the fact that you've even had the nerve to stay overnight at his place?"

"It's not at all what you think, Greg," Sam had quietly replied. "Claude was—"

"Did you stay overnight in his apartment?" Greg brutally interrupted, his anger and jealousy blanking out the truth shining from her eyes.

"Yes."

It had seemed totally inconceivable to Sam, as she boarded the plane for Reno two days later that one small word of admission could have such a devastating affect on her life.

Greg had refused to listen to anything, the warmth, the love she'd known in his arms, turning to ice before her very eyes. Sam had never known until today who had carried the tale to him. Now that she thought back, the missing pieces of the puzzle began to fall into place.

Monica Woods cherished her position as Greg's private secretary. Her single-minded goal in life had been to become his wife. That the man of her choice failed to reciprocate her feelings mattered little. Her position afforded her almost unlimited access to his comings and goings, as well as allowing her to be near him. It also gave her an excellent opportunity to keep a close watch on his social life.

"And later . . . on me as well," Sam muttered beneath her breath. Oh, God! she silently raged. How could I have been so stupid? Why didn't I put up more of a fight? Demand that Greg see Claude's doctor? Because, a tiny voice inside whispered, your pride was crushed. You couldn't risk the humiliation of having anyone else know what your husband thought of you.

30

Sam could well imagine Monica's delight in keeping Greg informed of his wife's almost daily visits to Claude's apartment, with the entire night Sam had spent on that one occasion being an added bonus. Of course, it would have considerably weakened the evidence for Sam's supposed infidelity if Monica had also revealed that Claude had been having an unusually difficult bout of asthma, and that during that same period Sam had gone by his apartment each afternoon to keep him abreast of the different jobs the firm was working on and their progress.

Or that Sam had ended up spending the night on that one occasion because she had found Claude fighting to get his breath, and had to rush him to the emergency room. The doctor had given him several injections, plus oral medication to be taken every few hours.

With Greg out of town Sam didn't hesitate to volunteer her services. Claude had no close relative, and her kind nature wouldn't allow her to desert him.

Sam gave a slight shake of her head and muttered a sharp expletive as she reflected on how easily she'd played into Monica's hands. She honestly assumed that after her marriage to Greg, the older woman would give up the chase. Now to suddenly learn that this hadn't been the case at all only served to strengthen her firm resolve to clear her name. Only she knew the real reason for her returning to New Orleans. Her surprise encounter today with Greg was the first step in the almost impossible task facing her.

By the time Sam reached the Faubourg Marigne area and the street where she lived, the shotgun cottage she'd recently purchased and the camelback addition only just completed, the bitter taste of regret was only slightly more palatable.

She remained in the car for several minutes, letting her gaze rest on the wrought-iron-trimmed front of the neat structure, its fresh coat of gray paint gleaming in the late afternoon sun. It was her very own, and she felt a deep sense of pride.

Originally the cottage had been of the straight shotgun design, one room leading directly into the other. However, with the help of an excellent carpenter recommended by Claude, Sam had added the second story in the form of what was locally known as a camelback. The addition started in the center of the roof and continued toward the rear, enabling Sam to add two bedrooms and another bath upstairs. Eventually the ground floor would consist of a combination living-dining room, a bath, plus a spacious kitchen and den.

Thus far the only structural change downstairs had involved sacrificing a long, narrow space for a hall that ran from the living room to the kitchen. Wallpaper, paint, and an enormous amount of hard work had resulted in a charming effect and one that Sam was very pleased with.

After another few minutes of silent approval of the

giant step she'd taken, Sam gathered up her purse and a package containing two new sets of playclothes for Elizabeth, and got out of the car.

She threw a quick glance toward the house to the right. Sometimes, if Mrs. Gautier happened to hear Sam's car, she would hold Elizabeth up to the window. Today, however, the lace curtains weren't moving.

Sam unlocked the door and dropped her things on a chair, then hurried back outside and across the narrow expanse of lawn to her neighbor's.

Before Mrs. Gautier could answer her knock, Sam was able to catch the excited squeals of her tiny daughter.

"I don't know how she does it." The plump, gray-headed woman smiled as she opened the door. "But every day about this time she starts getting fidgety."

Sam chuckled as she picked up Elizabeth and buried her face in the baby-soft skin of her neck. "Did you miss Mommy?" She drew back and looked into a miniature version of her own features.

"Mummy," Elizabeth chortled, rubbing her cheek against her mother's. "Go," she demanded, pointing with one chubby finger toward the door.

Sam and Mrs. Gautier both laughed at her imperious tone. "I don't think she's feeling too well today, Sam. She's been unusually quiet. I'd keep a close watch on her if I were you," the older woman advised.

Mrs. Gautier had been a godsend to Sam and Eliz-

33

abeth and had immediately taken them under her wing. Sam would have been lost without her reassuring support, not to mention the convenience of having a baby-sitter next door.

"I'll give her a nice warm bath and get her to bed early," Sam promised the surrogate grandmother, reaching for the small zippered case that contained Elizabeth's extra clothes and an assortment of toys.

At home Sam went first to the bright yellow-and-white kitchen, where she filled the kettle with water and set it on the stove. Next she fixed a quick meal for Elizabeth and buckled the active youngster into her highchair.

As Sam moved around the kitchen, talking to her daughter as she did so, it became quite obvious that Elizabeth was more interested in playing with her food than eating it. Added to her misery were the huge yawns that kept splitting her small face, the drooping of the thickly lashed lids. Instead of sitting and enjoying a cup of tea as she'd planned, Sam took pity on the little tyke.

A bath was accomplished hurriedly—minus the usual games that had become a nightly ritual. By the time Elizabeth was dried off, powdered, and snapped into a pair of pink pajamas, she'd given up. Sam couldn't help smiling as she tucked the soundly sleeping child into her youth bed, secured the railings, and turned on the soft glow of the night-light.

The remainder of the evening passed quickly. It was only after Sam was in bed that she allowed her thoughts to turn to Greg. For nearly three years she'd subjected herself to a rigid form of mental discipline where he was concerned. The hurt she'd suffered due to his unreasonable jealousy and his lack of faith in her had cut so deep that she'd either had to expunge it totally from her thoughts or let it destroy her.

Now to suddenly find out that Greg had been fed a pack of lies by Monica cast a different light on the situation. It struck her that she was also a different person now.

Her brief marriage to John Ewing had shown her that it wasn't necessary for two people to be head over heels in love with each other in order to be happy. It had been John's gentleness that appealed to Sam. There had been none of Greg's forcefulness, his aggressiveness about him.

Looking back on that time in her life, Sam could see now that she'd deliberately sought out a man as totally different from Greg as possible. If the excitement, the fire, was missing from the relationship, it hadn't mattered. Perhaps later it would have. She dismissed that thought. She wasn't omnipotent, besides . . . she felt a certain loyalty to John's memory. She wanted to believe they could have had a pleasant life—a good solid marriage. If it was not a carousel of exploding rockets as she'd known in Greg's arms, then so be it. She'd learned the hard way that one could be seriously burned by the fallout from such meteoric flights.

It had been after John's death, during the long, almost never-ending months of her solitary pregnancy, that Sam found her emotional orientation had swung full circle. At first she'd been shocked, even appalled, to find that, instead of her thoughts lingering on John . . . and the safe haven he'd created for her, it was Greg's face that haunted her.

Sam fought valiantly against this intrusion into her new life, but to no avail. There were moments when first awakening from dreams of Greg that she'd suffer a momentary lapse of memory. There would be a pleased smile on her face as she reached out with loving arms to . . . Greg? "Oh, God, no!" she would moan, burying her face in the pillow and weeping. "Oh, John. Please, please forgive me," she'd cry, her tortured voice resisting even then what would grow into a compulsion of such intensity as to consume her totally.

The next morning found Sam hard at work, her desk heaped with folders as well as several stacks of carpet samples and swatches of material.

"Heavens!" she muttered in a harassed undertone. "Either I'm the most disorganized person in the world, or this clutter is reproducing." She sat back in her chair, a frown pulling at her lips as she glanced at her watch.

The paperhangers should be well into the bedrooms at the Talton house. Since two other jobs were in the same general area, she decided to get out of the office for a while. For some strange reason the walls seemed to be closing in on her.

Several minutes later Sam walked through the front showroom in search of Libbie Thale, who was the receptionist, part-time salesperson, and general keeper of the flock. Without her watchful eye the place would be a shambles in less time than Sam cared to think about.

She was finally run to ground in the back, watching as workmen uncrated several small, expensive tables Claude had ordered.

"Libbie. I'll be out for at least two hours," she said, giving the attractive blonde a list of her planned stops. "If I get any calls, just take their numbers. I'll get back to them later."

"Will do, Sam. Have fun." The receptionist waved, then turned her eagle eye back to the work in progress.

During the time it took her to drive through the city to the exclusive Lakefront section, Sam found her thoughts drifting to Greg. She wondered who the current woman in his life was. That he wasn't the sort to remain celibate, she knew very well. Somehow she couldn't see their divorce changing that . . . and it annoyed her.

Quite irrationally, of course, she preferred to think of Greg as having suffered damnably after their divorce. And that, my dear, is a ridiculous fantasy! she thought derisively. Greg is not the suffering type.

Once his ego recovered, she was quite certain he'd returned to a normal life-style.

Women were attracted to him, and not always through any doing of his. He was tall; his black head usually towered above all the other men. He dressed with an eye toward the more traditional dark suits when working—faded denims, or whatever he grabbed first, when relaxing. But no matter what he wore, whatever the occasion, he wore it with a style that dictated its own terms.

He was the sort of man who could walk into a room full of people and be instantly noticed. His masculinity wasn't overly aggressive nor his sexuality overly overt. Yet he exuded a sensual promise in his every move that could have women from eighteen to eighty hanging on his every word with bated breath.

Sam sighed raggedly. Why should I be presumptuous enough to think my leaving him made even the slightest ripple in his life? Then, a mischievous smile broke through the brooding planes of her heart-shaped face. But I will make a ripple . . . no . . . nothing so gentle, Greg Howland. Before I'm through with you, you'll think you've been swamped by a tidal wave!

She turned into the driveway of the sprawling house with undue speed, the tires of the Volvo squealing protestingly. Get hold of yourself, she silently admonished. Crashing your car isn't likely to aid you in your pursuit of Greg. Judging from his reaction to you yesterday at lunch, your presence in New Orleans will definitely cause enough excitement without your ending up in plaster from toe to hip.

After parking behind a gray van belonging to Favret Interiors, Sam sat motionless, willing her thoughts to turn to a less unsettling subject than her ex-husband—preferably the eventual color scheme of the master bedroom she was about to visit.

With a pleased toss of her curly head she got out of the car and made her way to the spacious patio that ran the length of the back of the house.

There she could check the progress of the workmen. One young man was cutting the matting to go under the rich brown carpet, the edges of which could be seen in two large rolls placed some distance from the line of traffic.

"How's it going, Jim?" Sam greeted a redheaded, freckle-faced young man who was giving instructions to the two men helping him.

"Right on schedule, Sam. We should be through by three o'clock."

Sam continued her tour of inspection with Jim following close behind. He was the most dependable of Claude's employees, and Sam tried to get him for each of her jobs, knowing his sharp eye and conscientious effort would save her many hours of backtracking and endless worrying.

"Has Mr. Talton been by today?" Sam asked. She was anxious to have the friendly Texan see the results and gauge his reaction. The entire house had been redecorated for his mother, who would be moving to the city in less than six weeks.

"No, now that you mention it." He gave Sam a lopsided grin. "He usually 'just happens' to arrive about the same time as you do." Jim leaned against the doorjamb. "I wonder why?" His blandly innocent expression was not lost on Sam.

"Perhaps he's checking to see that he gets his money's worth." She grinned, knowing full well what he was getting at. She wasn't so silly that she didn't know when a man was interested in her, and Chace Talton certainly gave every indication of being just that. She turned back to Jim. "If the gentleman in question does stop by today, please tell him that barring any unforeseen complications—such as my murdering you—his house will be ready by Friday."

"I'd be happy to deliver that message, ma'am," he answered, giving an excellent imitation of the Texan's lazy drawl, "but I do believe you'll have that pleasure yourself. The gentleman in question just happens to be coming this way."

The entire time Sam was showing Chace Talton through the house, it became apparent that he was much more interested in her lovely smile, in the way the sun pouring in through the bare windows caught the sparkling highlights of her dark hair, the attractive curves of her slim body beneath the graceful lines of the wheat-colored skirt and matching long-sleeved silk blouse.

Sam was finding these attentions rather disconcerting, not to mention the knowing gleam in Jim's watchful eyes as he accompanied the pair in an unobtrusive fashion.

After viewing their progress and getting Sam's assurance that the job would be completed within the week, Chace surprised Sam by asking her to have dinner with him.

"I'm sorry, Mr. Talton, but I can't." She really meant just that. An evening out with a man as charming and attractive as Chace Talton would be a nice change.

"Chace, please. And if you won't have dinner with me, then how about a drink after work?"

Sam started to refuse that invitation as well and then changed her mind. "I'd like that."

As the day wore on she began to wonder if she'd been wise in accepting his invitation after all. Not that she was reading more into it than was really there. It was simply that her initial enthusiasm had vanished, which wasn't really surprising. She'd gone through the ritual too many times not to know that after the first fifteen minutes she'd find herself watching her date, silently comparing this unfortunate individual to Greg, and finding him sadly lacking.

After endless such occasions Sam had decided the waste of time wasn't worth the effort. However, since Chace Talton was a client, and such a nice one at that, she decided to wear her nicest smile and enjoy the time she'd be forced to spend with him . . . even if it killed her.

The men she'd gone out with since she had returned to New Orleans had been either old friends or acquaintances of Claire and Jacques, but it was always on a one-time basis. Sam shied away from anything that remotely resembled a steady relationship.

She'd even tried at one time to convince herself that it was because of Elizabeth, that she didn't want a succession of men parading through her young life. But that too proved a futile gesture. She was only using the little girl as an excuse.

It was slightly after five thirty when Sam entered the lounge, hesitating once she was inside, to let her eyes adjust to the dim lighting. She'd just gotten her bearings when she felt her elbow being clasped in a warm grip.

"You're prompt." Chace smiled as he led her to an incredibly small table. "I really expected you to stand me up."

"Why on earth would you expect that?" she asked, unable to meet his open gaze. Lord! Was she so easily read that a total stranger could accurately assess her thoughts?

"Well . . . you did seem to hesita   hen I asked you to meet me for a drink."

"Oh, that." Sam dismissed the subject with a casual wave of her hand. "I have a little girl. Sometimes it's not that easy to get a sitter."

That seemed to satisfy Chace, and the conversation turned to other topics, light and impersonal, the way Sam preferred it.

When the waitress finally made her way through the after-work crowd to their table, Sam, having already mentioned her preference to Chace, let her gaze wander around the room. It was a popular spot with people such as herself. There were as many unescorted women among the patrons as men.

"Do you come here often?" Chace asked as the waitress left and his attention was once again directed toward Sam.

"Occasionally. It's one of the few places I enjoy coming to, where I can relax. I also know the owner, Mike Kelly," she explained.

"Is he by any chance that huge mountain standing over by the bar?"

Sam turned and looked in the direction he indicated, chuckling at the surly expression on the bulldog features of the proprietor. "The one and the same. Don't be fooled by his looks. Actually he's a pussycat."

Sam asked Chace about his work, having decided it would be a safe topic, then sat back and listened . . . and listened!

After thirty minutes or so had gone by without his showing the slightest inclination of slowing down, she found herself sipping on her second drink and becoming increasingly bored with the subject of computers.

In her experience all a computer signified was the

unholy mixup of her gasoline credit card or her various department store charge accounts. Even her checking account had fallen victim to the monster. Now, here she was, seated across from a . . . a keeper of one of those very monsters, literally bored stiff by his incessant ramblings.

Relief came in a manner that was most unexpected.

A movement in Sam's left peripheral range caused her to look casually toward the entrance. Had Chace not been so wound up with his story, he would have noticed the visible start she gave as her gaze became fixed on one of the four men who had just entered the lounge. Greg Howland was laughing at some remark made by Sean, his features relaxed and carefree. The other men that made up the foursome were strangers to Sam.

Instead of turning away once she'd seen him, Sam continued to stare. It was as though her eyes had suddenly become a separate entity, with a mind of their own. It was her first opportunity since she had left Greg to observe him without his being aware of it.

There was the same loose-limbed casualness in his stance, a casualness Sam knew was capable of galvanizing into swift, direct action without any noticeable change in his expression. He was vitally alert, mentally and physically, at all times. She knew those eyes, as emerald-green as her own, could take a person apart and put him (or her) back together again

44

without ever hinting that he was doing so. But the thing that intrigued her most was the sameness of him. There wasn't the tiniest particle of difference in his face, the determined chin and jaw as implacable as ever.

CHAPTER THREE

Suddenly her surreptitious appraisal became anything but that, with Greg turning as though on cue from some invisible prompter . . . staring straight into her eyes.

Rather than engaging in a visual battle she could in no way win, Sam forced her gaze away from Greg's, letting it touch on each member of his party, then back to Chace.

"It's really a fascinating field," he remarked expansively, bringing his lengthy summation to an end.

"I'm sure it is," Sam murmured, knowing she would never be able to sit calmly with Greg in the same room, his eyes burning into her back.

"How about a refill?" Chace asked.

"No . . . no thanks. I've already had two. Actually, Chace, I'm afraid I have to be going, it's—"

"Why, Chace Talton, you sly dog," Greg's voice was louder than usual in order to be heard over the noise. "You didn't tell me your appointment was with Samantha."

The next few minutes were never exactly clear in Sam's mind. All she was sure of was Chace warmly greeting Greg and his friends, and asking them to join them, then momentary confusion as another table was shoved in place along with additional chairs. When the scramble ended, Sam found herself neatly sandwiched between Greg and Sean, with Chace at the opposite end of the table.

"Hands off, Greg," the lanky Texan drawled. "I saw her first." His remark drew good-natured chuckles from the others.

"Not so, Chace. Samantha and I go way back," Greg said easily. "Why don't you concentrate on selling Jake and Fred one of those complicated computer systems like the one I bought? I'll take care of this young lady." He subjected Sam to a heavy-lidded scrutiny that brought a flush slowly creeping upward from the slim column of her neck to stain her face.

Damn you! Sam silently cursed, though once again the other men thought his remark was amusing and laughed. That is, all but Sean. He was watching the entire proceedings with the merest of grins curving the sensuous mouth that was so like Greg's. He also knew Sam well enough to know that she wouldn't tolerate that sort of treatment for very long.

Chace, faced with not one but two warm . . . breathing potential clients, bowed to Greg's suggestion, with an apologetic grin thrown toward Sam.

"Well, now that we've settled that little matter. Tell me, Samantha, what have you been doing with yourself?" Greg asked facetiously, leaning forward, his forearms resting on the edge of the table, his face uncomfortably close.

"None of your damned business," Sam muttered in a low furious voice, gritting her teeth in frustration. The nerve of him! The unbelievable nerve of him!

"Tsk, tsk," he admonished. "How unladylike."

"Being a lady has nothing to do with this ridiculous farce and you know it," she hissed, under cover of the loud talk going on all around them. "Your implication that we are old friends is ludicrous."

"I see," Greg remarked acidly. He picked up the glass the waitress set before him and raised it to his lips, his eyes watching her over the rim. "Would you rather I'd said that you're my ex-wife? That our divorce came about as a result of your taking a lover while I was still your husband?"

For one incredible moment Sam thought she would faint from the rage that surged through her body. Even her fingertips prickled with the ice-hot emotion that overwhelmed her senses. Instead of allowing the tears of anger that had immediately rushed to the corners of her eyes to overflow, she willed them back. She met Greg's flinty gaze with her own equally unyielding one.

"The only moral lapse I was ever guilty of, Greg, was failing to see you for the insufferably narrow-minded, jealous bastard you really are." She came to her feet, the chair almost toppling over from the force. "Nice seeing you, Sean," she ground out, thinking, rather hysterically, that he must surely be tired of hearing that silly statement from her. She nodded briefly toward Chace, then rushed for the door, oblivious to the curious looks she was receiving.

Just as she reached the street and started toward the parking lot, she felt a heavy hand drop to her shoulder.

"Not so fast, Samantha," Greg growled, falling into step with her, his fingers biting into her skin as she tried to pull away.

No match for him physically, she tried a verbal attack. "What now, Greg? More insults? Are you disappointed that Sean was your only audience back there?"

"No, dammit, that's not it at all," he thundered, forced to come to an abrupt halt as Sam reached her car and began searching through her purse for her keys. "I came to apologize," he finished in a gravelly voice.

Sam jerked her head up, unable to hide her surprise at such an admission. She stared into his face,

49

at the frown that was stamped across the rugged features, the pulsation of the tiny muscle in his cheek. For one insane moment she was tempted to laugh. She was faced with this giant of a man . . . the same man she'd shared a part of her life with. He'd just insulted her, and now he stood before her, his apology still ringing in her ears, looking as though he was about to explode!

Sam was tempted to taunt him further, but something held her back. "Apology accepted," she said instead. "Now if you'll excuse, I have to rush. It's way past time to pick up my daughter."

"I know," Greg again surprised her by saying. "I thought you'd forgotten her when I walked in back there and saw you with Talton."

So . . . he knew about Elizabeth, did he? Jacques had indeed been busy, Sam thought nastily. On the other hand she found she liked the idea of Greg knowing about her daughter. "I'm not likely to forget about Elizabeth," she said softly.

Greg shrugged. "It's not that uncommon these days. I'd venture to guess that over half the women in that lounge are content to let someone else take care of their children."

Sam shook her head in confusion, wondering where this ridiculous conversation was headed—but not in the least eager for it to end. "I assure you that being a mother is very important to me. The time I spend away from my daughter certainly isn't going to do her any harm."

Greg stared at the heart-shaped face, his expression an inscrutable mask. Only his eyes held a hint of the softness, the gentleness Sam knew that he was capable of. "I'm glad to hear that. Somehow the image of you preferring a heavy social life didn't seem in character."

A rueful smile touched Sam's lips. Again she wasn't certain if she'd been complimented or insulted. On an impulse she said, "Why don't you come over some night and see Elizabeth?" She extended the invitation before her negative thoughts could convince her that he wouldn't accept. She wanted Greg to see that she *was* a good mother, as well that another man had loved her enough to want her to be the mother of his child.

"I'd like to," he said without the slightest pause. "How about this evening?"

"Er . . . I'm not . . . it's—" she stammered before he interrupted her.

"Trying to wiggle out already?" he taunted, leaning one sinewy arm on the roof of the Volvo, his other hand tucked into the waistband of his trousers. There was a rakish nonchalance to his leaning stance, a wickedly devilish gleam in his green eyes.

Sam felt the old familiar thump, thump of her heart as she bravely bore the full brunt of his most charming attention. "Not at all," she replied huskily, doing her darndest to keep her glance from straying over the slant of broad shoulder under the suit jacket, the muscular outline of his chest tapering down to a narrow waist and lean hips. The taut pull of the dark fabric of his trousers over his strong, firm thighs gave her a breathless feeling that was humiliating.

"What time?"

"What?" Sam looked blankly at him, not really hearing the words, merely the sound of his deep voice.

"You invited me to visit you and Elizabeth. I accepted," he answered, reiterating their conversation with patient amusement at her flustered air. "What time may I call on you?" he repeated, the corners of his mouth twitching suspiciously.

"Seven thirty," Sam muttered as the enormity of what she'd done swept over her.

Greg moved back from the car, reached for the handle, and opened the door. Sam slid in beneath his arm, which brought her disturbingly close to his chest. The scent of his spicy shaving lotion teased her nose, causing her to fumble as she went to insert the key in the ignition.

"Are you sure you can drive? You haven't had too much to drink, have you?" Greg asked darkly.

"No," Sam assured in a saccharine voice. "Sorry to disappoint you, but I haven't added alcoholism to my long list of vices." She flashed him her coldest smile, knowing from previous experience that it was guaranteed to enrage him, then roared out of the parking lot.

All during the drive home and later, after she'd gotten Elizabeth from Mrs. Gautier's, Sam kept asking herself if she had moved too quickly, then just as swiftly dismissed the idea. Perhaps she could have used a more subtle approach—quizzed Jacques on Greg's favorite haunts, even had Claire invite him to dinner. But rational thinking where Greg was concerned had never been Sam's strong suit.

"And like a damn fool, I always manage to let him know," she muttered as she lifted Elizabeth from her high chair and began cleaning up the mess made by the active toddler.

Greg had entered Sam's life like a great storm, sweeping aside anyone or anything that stood between him and his goal of having her for himself. Their marriage had been like the merging of two smoldering coals that blazed into a raging fire when combined.

Even their arguments, their disagreements, were just as volatile, since both had tempers that needed little provocation to erupt. It was Sam who learned control, and eventually Greg did too, to a degree. But there was one facet of his personality that remained unchanged . . . his uncontrollable jealousy.

Now, looking back, Sam could see how Monica's lies must have devastated him. And I was so stupid, she thought grimly. Instead of staying and getting to the bottom of the lies, I ran. Well not anymore, she vowed, not anymore.

Sam was like a small tornado in her faded denims and cotton T-shirt, her feet snug in a pair of thick crew socks as she darted from one room to the next

53

. . . straightening a cushion here, an ashtray there. Elizabeth, clad in her pink pajamas, followed closely behind. Sam wanted everything in perfect order when Greg arrived. Her pride wouldn't allow it to be otherwise.

The one thing that most annoyed her was a large wicker trunk on one side of the living room. It rested on a layer of newspapers, waiting for a final coat of white paint. Sam paused in her cleaning frenzy and stared balefully at this object, wondering if she had time to drag it down the hall to the kitchen. Deciding that she did, she hurried over and lifted the lid, placing the can of paint and the brush inside. She then grasped the handle on the end nearest her and began tugging and pulling.

Elizabeth, thinking her mother had found a new form of transportation solely for her own private enjoyment, immediately tried to climb on top. Instead she slipped backward, banging her head on the edge of the coffee table. This resulted in a howl of protest from the little girl, more from having her plans thwarted than actual pain.

Sam smiled at her daughter's antics and picked her up, holding her warm little body close and rubbing the back of the curly head. "I'm sorry, sweetheart," she crooned.

Sensing the sympathetic note in her mother's voice, Elizabeth restrained her outpouring of grief by several decibels and leveled off to a pitiful snubbing noise.

Sam held her a few minutes longer, and was just on the point of putting her down when the doorbell sounded.

"Oh, dear," she murmured, eyeing the trunk, which was now sitting smack in the middle of the room. "Now it really does stick out like a sore thumb. Oh, well." She shrugged, walked over to the door, and opened it.

Greg was leaning against the wall, still in the same clothes he'd had on earlier, one forefinger positioned over the small black button. "I thought for a moment you were in the back and didn't hear the bell." He grinned lazily, pushing his considerable bulk away from the wall and stepping inside. It was then that Sam saw the large package he was carrying, the name of a well-known toy shop written across it.

"I heard you," Sam replied, "but Elizabeth was doing her mountain-goat routine and had a slight accident." She smiled down at her daughter, who was subjecting Greg to a thorough examination.

"Hello, Elizabeth." Greg smiled at the little girl, a gentleness in his manner that Sam had never seen before. "Would you like to see what I've got in this bag?" He held the light-blue-and-white checked bag with the gold lettering up so that she could see it.

Not being of the strongest character where a man was concerned, Elizabeth was doubly swayed by a man who was holding a package that promised untold treasures. Greg chuckled as the tiny imp gave him a huge smile and reached out with both arms for him.

He took her and settled her in the crook of his arm. "Mmmmm," he laughingly mused. "I can see right now that I'll have to teach you not to be so easily swayed by nicely wrapped packages." He stepped around the trunk and walked over to the pale-green-and-tan-patterned sofa and sat down.

Sam stood uncertainly in the middle of the room, unaware of her duties as hostess. Somewhere in the dos and don'ts of proper etiquette she was certain there must be a chapter on how to entertain an ex-husband. Unfortunately she'd never seen it. What on earth did one use as an icebreaker? There were the obvious facts one knew about a former spouse, such as taste in clothes, favorite foods. On the other hand the merest slip of the tongue could easily bring back memories that would be best forgotten.

"Why don't you offer me a cup of coffee, Samantha, and stop looking so nervous, mmmmm?" Greg broke into her painful mental gyrations. "Just think of me as an old friend . . . Claude Favret, for example." He gave her a measured look before turning his attention back to Elizabeth and the toys she was unearthing from the large package.

At the mention of Claude's name Sam forgot all about her uneasiness. She spun around and grabbed the trunk and pulled it down the hall, not caring that she'd have to touch up the corners and sides after she had banged against the walls like that.

So much for the ridiculous notion of treating Greg like a guest, her insane concern over how best to put him at ease, she fumed as she stashed the trunk in one corner of the roomy kitchen. He's still as pig-headed and stubborn as he was three years ago!

How a grown man, supposedly mature, could have been duped by the likes of Monica, and still believe her was beyond Sam's power to comprehend. There had been moments during the three times she'd seen Greg, in the last two days, when it had occurred to Sam that in spite of her deep love for him she'd like nothing better than to clobber him over the head with a baseball bat!

She stalked over to the counter and opened a cupboard and got down the can of coffee. Next, she spooned the proper amount into the coffeepot, added water, and switched it on.

Instead of returning to the living room, she decided to wash the few dishes that were still in the sink and give herself time to simmer down. She leaned against the counter and watched the hot water as it poured into the sink, creating a small mountain of suds.

Common sense told her that in spite of her obvious annoyance with Greg if she were ever to establish any sort of relationship with him, his acceptance of Elizabeth was of paramount importance. His pointed references to her daughter, plus his warm greeting, gave Sam cause to believe that Elizabeth would be one point on which she and Greg wouldn't disagree.

So why the tears? she asked herself as she wiped at her eyes with the back of one hand—only to have the tiny voice inside her whisper back, because you're grieving for the child you begged Greg to let you have . . . for the lies and deceit that were responsible for destroying a love you thought was indestructible.

Sam thought back earlier to when she had invited Greg to come over and see Elizabeth. She had an idea he was perfectly aware that she was using her daughter as bait. The simple truth was . . . she wanted to see him, wanted him to see her in her home, as a mother. Well, now she was getting her wish, and for the first time in a long time, she found herself looking forward to spending time with a man, the one man with the power to banish the haunting memories that had become a part of her life.

Once the dishes were taken care of, Sam reached for a brightly colored mug, filled it with coffee, added a spoon of sugar, and stirred it. She was halfway to the living room before it hit her that the entire procedure had been carried out by rote. There was a possibility that Greg's taste might have changed.

Great! she thought nastily. I hope he's taking it unsweetened. If so, he can damn well get it for himself. That will teach him to throw Claude Favret's name in my face at every turn.

The sight that greeted Sam when she entered the room stemmed the acid flow of words ready to burst from her lips. Instead she found it difficult to dislodge the huge lump that rose in her throat. Greg, his dark head bent close to Elizabeth's, was reading from a book he'd brought. Each page depicting a colorful picture of a farm animal, complete with the appropriate sound when one pressed a particular spot on the page.

Elizabeth, fairly bursting with excitement, was sprawled across Greg's lap as though she'd known him all her life instead of a scant thirty minutes.

"Here's your coffee." Sam spoke more stiffly than she meant to, not wanting him to see just how moved she was by the touching scene. She placed the mug on the coffee table, then walked over and sat down in one of the chairs facing the sofa. Greg looked up at her, noting the taut features of her face, the rigid set of her lips, before continuing with the story.

"Moo, Mommy!" Elizabeth exclaimed seconds later, one plump finger finding and pushing the correct spot.

"I see, darling," Sam smiled, masking the sense of depression she was feeling. She refused to meet Greg's probing gaze, concentrating instead on the assortment of toys on the sofa. "You shouldn't have been so extravagant," she told him in a subdued voice.

"Elizabeth doesn't think so, do you, princess?" Greg smiled at the dimpled moppet perched on his lap. "Is it time for her to go to bed?" he asked, looking at Sam over the curly head.

"Yes, it is," she answered, getting to her feet and

covering the small space from chair to sofa. "Tell Greg good night, sweetie. It's way past your bedtime."

Elizabeth vigorously shook her head, burrowing her small body against Greg's broad chest and flinging her arms around his neck.

"Is it all right if I tuck her in?" he asked, as surprised as Sam by the child's actions.

"Certainly," she murmured, feeling a little betrayed by how easily he'd won over her daughter and quite happy that he and Elizabeth felt no restraint in their newfound relationship.

Sam led the way into the smaller of the two bedrooms that she had done over temporarily for Elizabeth. The walls were covered with wallpaper in a tiny blue flowered design on a white background. A matching coverlet on the bed with a white dust ruffle and frilly white curtains at the window cast a cheery glow over the room.

She turned back the covers and positioned two stuffed animals on the bed. Sam watched as Greg placed her daughter between the fuzzy dog and the bedraggled teddy bear. He tucked the little girl and the animals in, smiling and talking in a soft voice as he did so.

He leaned down and kissed one rosy cheek. "I'll come back and visit you again real soon," he promised. "Good night, princess."

Elizabeth gave him a sleepy smile, pleased as punch with her newest friend.

After making sure the guard rails were in place on the bed, Sam turned off the bedside lamp and switched on the night-light. She gave a final pat to the covers and then followed Greg from the room.

Back in the living room, she started toward the chair she'd previously occupied, only to feel Greg's hand on her arm. An electric shock ran through her body at his touch.

"Why not join me on the sofa?" he asked huskily. "I really don't think you're afraid I'll pounce on you, are you?"

Sam raised her head and met his amused gaze. She shrugged. "No. Frankly, I don't recall that you were ever forced to resort to such drastic measures." She followed the gentle pressure of his hand and sank into the softness of the cushions. She drew her feet beneath her and turned so that she was facing him. When he lowered his tall frame, it was not at the opposite end of the sofa, as she'd hoped, but exactly in the middle!

His proximity was viewed with a strange sense of excitement by Sam, the pounding of her heart pointing out a fact that grew more apparent each day . . . she loved Greg.

CHAPTER FOUR

"Aren't you having any coffee?" Greg asked, raising the mug to his lips.

"No. It keeps me awake." Sam smiled. "Would you like yours warmed up? I made six cups."

"Later . . ." That one word caused a peculiar thrill to run through Sam, and at the same time quelled the apprehension she'd felt that after seeing Elizabeth he'd immediately bolt for the door.

"I like your home, Samantha. You've really done a nice job on it. Who's doing the work for you?"

She smiled. "You're looking at her. Of course, I had to hire a carpenter to add the camelback, as well as adding the temporary walls to accommodate the hallway. As for the painting and papering, I've done most of that myself. I really can't afford to have someone come in and do it."

"I see," Greg replied in a clipped voice, settling his broad shoulders against the cushioned back of the sofa, his long legs stretched out in front of him. "Why hasn't Claude come to your rescue? I'd think he'd be only too happy to assist you." His head turned, his burning gaze almost searing her with its heat.

"For an alleged financial genuis, as well as a top-notch engineer, you baffle me with your continued stupidity," Sam told him in a firm voice. "Hasn't it occurred to you yet that if I'd been as enamored with Claude . . . and he with me . . . as you seem to think, we would have been married by now?"

"Stranger things have happened," Greg replied laconically, refusing to budge an inch.

"Then if you still think I was unfaithful to you, why are you here? Have you concluded in that pea-sized brain of yours that since I'm an unfaithful bitch, you'd get some vicarious thrill by visiting me and my daughter? Did you hope there would be a succession of men parading through, that my telephone would be ringing off the wall from satisfied customers wanting my services again?" Her voice was shrill and trembling as she hurled the questions at him.

"No, dammit, I didn't think any such thing." Greg glared at her, and he had gone quite pale under her attack. He stared at her, his mouth a rigid slash across the granite hardness of his face. Suddenly he reached out and grasped her by her shoulders, hauling her against him, his mouth only a hairbreadth from hers. "I came here tonight for this," he murmured, his lips claiming hers in a kiss that could only be described as mind-shattering!

Sam met his assault with an equally angry response, enraged that he would assume she'd be willing to surrender so easily to him after those vile accusations, accusations that had caused her months . . . even years of intense agony.

Greg met this determined resistance with an iron resolve borne of his own frustrations, which equaled Sam's. In spite of her anger and her inner torment, Sam could feel her own resolutions to remain aloof from the conflicting emotions he was creating within her crumbling into nothing, leaving her frightened and vulnerable. This was not what she had intended when she had invited him, to fall willingly into his arms. But where Greg was concerned, common sense had never been her strong point either.

When his tongue challenged her own in the teasing game of touch, taste, then skillfully darted back to explore the familiar dark sweetness, Sam reluctantly accepted.

Her lips moved sensuously beneath Greg's, coaxing, reacquainting themselves with part of him that had given her so much pleasure. With a boldness arising from thirsting desire, Sam withdrew the tip of her tongue from the heated warmth of his mouth and began to trace the line of his lower lip in a light, flicking curve.

When Greg attempted to put a stop to this delicious punishment, Sam let the edges of her teeth nibble at the lip she'd so lovingly teased, and quickly began the erotic soothing of the spot by caressing it with her lips.

Suddenly Greg could bear it no longer. One large hand slid upward over her rib cage, the rigid tips of her breasts, and clasped her chin in an attempt to still the smoldering flame that her mouth was awakening within him.

Sam knew instinctively the state of his arousal. . . . Part of her was reveling in her ability to bring him to such a fever pitch of excitement, the other concerned exclusively with her own needs. When she felt his lips on the sensitive throbbing pulse of her throat, she was unable to stifle the low purring sounds that escaped from her parted lips.

His hands slid unerringly beneath the unrestrained edge of the T-shirt she wore, capturing the fullness of her breasts. Sam felt the gentle pressure of his hands on the creamy globes, the slight abrasiveness of his palms creating a friction that brought a gasp of desire from her that was caught and absorbed by Greg's lips.

She had no idea how long it lasted nor was she aware of Greg pushing up the T-shirt and baring her breasts, his tongue licking the roseate tips, his lips tugging as he nibbled and gently nipped at that sensi-

tive part of her anatomy. It was only when all movement from him ceased and Sam felt him easing backward from her, that it occurred to her just how
vulnerable she was, sprawled in total abandon across
his muscular thighs.

She briefly closed her eyes, hating herself because
of this weakness she had for Greg, knowing it would
merely reinforce his opinion of her, blotting out his
ability to see her for what she really was—a loving
mother, a devoted wife.

At her feeble attempts to cover herself Greg
looked down into her passion-kissed face, a curious
glitter in his own emerald eyes. "Does that answer
your question about why I came?" he asked hoarsely,
pushing her hands out of the way and smoothing the
shirt back in place. Instead of helping her up, he
continued to hold her, one arm finding its way across
her chest, his palm cupping the mound beneath the
thin material as she stilled burned with indignation.

"When I saw you at Antoine's yesterday, I was
like a man who's been poleaxed. I knew you'd returned to New Orleans and that you were living
here." He gave a humorless sort of laugh. "I've even
driven by here, seen you in the yard, bringing Elizabeth home from next door. But meeting you face to
face . . . I knew I couldn't wait any longer. If we
hadn't met at Kelly's this afternoon, I'm afraid I
would have surprised you one evening by arriving
unannounced."

"Why, Greg?" Sam asked curiously, slowly willing herself back to normal, restraining the coil of anger and desire in the pit of her stomach that was threatening to explode. She had wanted Greg at that moment, so much so that she was still aching from it, but she hated the power he had over her.

"Who the hell knows?" he rasped. "I sure don't."

"You still don't trust me, do you?" She read the silent accusation in the tortured depths of his eyes.

"I don't want to talk about it," he growled, exhaling loudly, his nostrils narrowing, his lips compressed. "But I do want to see you again. Will you have dinner with me tomorrow evening?" He stared at her, his hand straying to the mass of soft curls, threading his fingers through the silken thickness.

"Yes," Sam unhesitatingly answered. She would rather it were with no distrust between them, but nothing on earth could stop her from seeing him, regardless of his reasons.

"About seven?" At her nod he asked, "Is there any trouble with a sitter?"

"No, I'm sure Mrs. Gautier will keep Elizabeth," she softly murmured.

"Good. By the way, I'm very fond of your daughter," he remarked casually. "I find myself quite pleased that there's no father to whisk her away on alternate weekends." The stark cruelty of his words brought a gasp of startled disbelief from Sam.

"Don't," he warned, placing a finger against her lips, already parted in readiness to protest at such a horrible admission. "I know how it sounds, Samantha. Perhaps later . . . I'll feel ashamed. At the moment, all I can see is you in another man's arms, the heat of that passion creating that beautiful little girl in the next room. But don't worry, I don't hate her. How can I? She's exactly like you—what our child could have been."

Later in bed, as she twisted and turned in an attempt to get comfortable, Sam found herself still trembling from her physical encounter with Greg, as well as his cruel reference to John.

God! she thought miserably. I had no idea how deeply his hostilities ran. Obviously he has similar feelings toward Claude . . . probably more so. Knowing Greg as she did, she could well imagine how he might resent her marriage, the fact that she'd been happy with another man to the extent of having borne his child. But she'd honestly been shocked at the depth of his resentment. Now she realized exactly what Claude had been alluding to when he recounted his visit with Greg. The only thing that surprised her now that she'd actually heard the way he'd talked about John, was that he hadn't beaten poor Claude to a pulp.

She forced her thoughts to turn back to her work, a far more soothing prospect for a good night's sleep than the complications she foresaw in the future with Greg.

Friday was hectic. The wallpaper for a job that was due to start on the following Monday didn't arrive, necessitating a call to the manufacturer. They were temporarily out of the particular pattern she had ordered, but would ship it as soon as possible. The draperies that were to finish the Talton house couldn't be hung because the head seamstress was out with the flu. Claude had come down with a severe case of bronchitis, and Sam was slowly pulling out her hair.

She and Libbie stared at each other across the latter's desk, both wanting nothing more than to throw up their hands and walk . . . leaving the confusion behind.

"This is turning into an absolute nightmare," Sam groaned, raising one slim hand and running it through her tousled hair as she looked down at the cluttered desk, especially the schedule for the coming week.

"I agree. If it wasn't for Jim, we'd be in even worse shape," Libbie wisely pointed out.

"How true, how true," Sam mused as she reached for a pencil and scribbled further instructions for the young man. "After he sees this"—waving the sheet of paper she held—"he might resign."

"Perish the thought!" Libbie shuddered. "Claude is an absolute genius when it comes to decorating, but without an army of assistants, especially Jim, he'd be lost."

Sam agreed, up to a point. However, it was Claude's ability to come up with spectacular ideas that accounted for his success, plus his innate gift for surrounding himself with a staff that was capable of carrying out his ideas. It was one of the many aspects that set Favret Interiors apart from other decorating firms.

If things got hectic, as was the case at the moment, then it was up to the staff to cope. After all, Sam reflected, Claude wasn't stingy when it came to salaries.

"If at all possible," she told Libbie, "I'd like to leave for about an hour sometime this afternoon. I'm going out to dinner this evening, and I think I'll splurge on that green dress we saw last week."

"Wow!" Libbie exclaimed. "It must be someone special. That dress can only be described as dangerous."

"Yes." Sam grinned. "It is, isn't it?"

"Do I know this exciting individual? He's obviously important, to get you to rush out and buy something new."

"Greg Howland," Sam replied, then laughed at Libbie's look of incredulity.

"*The* Greg Howland? Your former . . . I mean your ex-hu—"

"Yes, yes, and yes." Sam's green eyes were alit with amusement.

"Oh . . . I see," Libbie murmured, unsure of how to react in face of this startling information. "Is it serious?"

"That," Sam retorted saucily, "is a good question. Until two days ago it had been three years since I'd seen him."

70

"You'll have to forgive me, Sam, but I've no idea what to say," Libbie confessed, a comical twist to her mouth. She'd been around during the separation and subsequent divorce, and knew the story well. She also remembered how broken up Sam had been and had no desire to see the same thing happen again.

"That makes two of us. At least . . . oh, it's difficult to explain. I suppose it has something to do with pride. For three years I've been made to feel guilty about something I didn't do, and it hasn't been a comfortable feeling at all. I want Greg to believe in me, Lib. It's become an obsession with me."

"Just be careful, honey. Sometimes it's easy to confuse vindication with revenge. I can certainly understand what you want to do, but Greg Howland. . . ." Libbie shook her head. "He's a law unto himself, Sam. This time he could quite easily destroy you."

Sam thought of that warning a good while later as she drove to a small, exclusive dress shop she patronized occasionally. Libbie would have been surprised to know that she'd actually hit upon Sam's *original* idea. At first she had wanted revenge. She spent every waking hour thinking of ways to make Greg suffer as she had, dreaming of the ultimate moment when she would see him brought low. But as time wore on she was forced to face the truth. She wanted to prove to him how wrong he'd been about Claude. She also had to admit that his opinion of her took precedence over any thoughts of revenge. She wanted his love, wanted it desperately.

71

Last night had not only proved to Sam that there could never be any other man for her but Greg . . . it had surprised, even shocked her that Greg had openly admitted he'd been watching her house, had seen her with Elizabeth.

There was a sinking feeling in the pit of her stomach as she was forced to admit that almost three years of self-imposed exile, her second marriage, and countless anguished thoughts hadn't helped in the least to banish Greg from her heart.

Her only moment of victory had come when she remembered the look of longing she'd seen in his eyes in the heat of their lovemaking. But why? she asked herself. Why would he even want to be around me, feeling as he does? Even though Claude had gone to him and reassured him that the story of their "affair" was merely a vicious lie on Monica's part, Greg still thought the worst of her. She could see it in every unguarded look he sent her, in each derisive remark he made about Claude.

She heaved a great sigh of frustration, no closer to understanding him now than three years ago. Hopefully, having dinner with him would shed some light on *his* reasons for wanting to see her again. Could it be, Sam asked herself, that Greg too had had three years in which to plot his revenge?

"It's perfect," enthused the clerk as she stood back and observed the green dress that softly clung to

Sam's slender curves. "A perfect size eight. And it exactly matches the green of your eyes."

"It does look nice," Sam agreed, turning first one way, then the other in front of the large three-way mirror.

The dress was quite simple in design, the bodice unadorned except for a wide three-layered ruffled collar that crisscrossed in front to the waist, forming a deep vee that exposed the dusky valley between her breasts. The sheer skirt was fully gathered, with an underskirt of taffeta lending just the proper amount of crispness.

Sam's lips pursed thoughtfully as she did a swift calculation of her bank balance and the large gap the dress would leave. But in spite of the outrageous price, she turned smiling to the clerk. "I'll take it."

There was an excited air about her as she parked the blue Volvo. She gathered up the box containing the dress and her purse, and hurried inside. Her eyes quickly scanned the showroom for Libbie, wanting to show off her new finery. Not finding her, Sam walked back to the large workroom. "Sophie, have you seen Libbie?" she asked one of several graduate students from a local university who worked at the shop in the afternoons.

"I think she's in Mr. Favret's office, Mrs. Ewing. Do you want me to get her for you?"

"Oh, no." Sam smiled. "I'll find her. Thank you, though." She turned and had started down the light-gray-carpeted hall toward the offices when the door to Claude's office opened and Libbie stepped out, her hands at her right ear as she replaced a gold earring.

"Sam!" she exclaimed. "Thank goodness. I just had Mrs. Rainer on the line from the dress shop, hoping to catch you."

"What's wrong?"

"Mrs. Gautier called. Elizabeth is running a high fever."

Sam leaned against the wall, a sigh of frustration escaping her. "Oh, no, not again."

"Tonsils again?" Libbie asked, concerned.

"Probably so. She didn't eat well last night or this morning. I should have known there was something wrong." She grinned, albeit ruefully. "Oh, well . . . the best laid plans of mice and men . . ." She moaned, indicating the box she was carrying under one arm.

A quick peek at her watch told her that Elizabeth's pediatrician wouldn't be in his office this late, so that meant calling him and having him meet her at the hospital.

"Can I help?" Libbie offered, following Sam into her office.

"Please . . ." Sam rattled off a telephone number as she thumbed through her personal desk directory for the doctor's number. "That's Greg's private line. Will you call and tell him that dinner's off, and why?"

"Of course. You just scoot home and get that baby taken care of. I'll see to Mr. Howland." Libbie chuckled at how blasé she sounded, when in actuality she found Greg to be quite intimidating. Sexy as sin, but still intimidating.

"I'm afraid your diagnosis is correct, Sam. It's another flareup with her tonsils." Tim Calder confirmed Sam's suspicions as he peered into Elizabeth's mouth, angling the tongue depressor in order to get a better view. "Her ears are red as well," he pronounced, giving them a quick look.

After completing his examination, he stepped aside so that Sam could cuddle the fretting child. "We'll get her started on medication right away. You know the routine by now." He sighed. "Be sure and keep her quiet."

"Of course." Sam smiled wearily. "One day I think I'll give you that same advice, then leave her in your care. It sounds simple until you actually have to do it."

A short time later, on her way home with Elizabeth asleep beside her, Sam couldn't help smiling as she remembered Jacques's look of disgust when he'd overheard her and Claire discussing Tim Calder. It had been one of the few times she'd agreed to have dinner with them.

Sam mentioned that Tim had asked her out. Claire, sensing, but not really understanding her peculiar reticence with regard to men, had merely smiled, but refrained from asking why Sam had refused.

Jacques, however, was unpracticed in the gentle art of minding his own business. He began a lengthy monologue on the excellent qualifications of Tim Calder, as well as two or three other well-established individuals he'd introduced Sam to.

Out of deference to Claire, Sam endured her brother's asinine interference for what she considered a reasonable period of time, after which she told him in blunt fashion to mind his own business!

Sam grimaced at Jacques's efforts to see her "safely" married. To his way of thinking it was unnatural for her to be away from Elizabeth all day. Marriage would put a stop to this gross neglect of his niece, and at the same time provide the youngster with a fatherly influence.

That his sister failed to share his cold commonsense approach led to a number of arguments between them, with the result that Sam had kept her visits with her only relatives to a minimum.

She hadn't returned to New Orleans just to allow herself to become a puppet at the mercy of Jacques's skillful manipulations. It wasn't difficult for her to imagine the shock on his aristocratic face if she were to tell him of the one man she did want. For to Jacques's narrow-minded way of thinking, Greg wouldn't touch Sam with a ten-foot pole!

She thought back over the few months of her marriage to John, comparing it with the year she and Greg had been together. It was like placing a pearl next to a flaming emerald, its many facets catching the light and blinding the beholder with its fire and brilliance.

Having sampled both, Sam knew with certainty that she would never allow herself to be pushed into another relationship based merely on respect. Greg had been and always would be a vital part of her life.

Instead of parking on the street, Sam turned into the alley behind her house and stopped the car. With a sick child, she wouldn't be going out much over the weekend.

After Elizabeth was taken care of and tucked in bed, Sam put on the kettle. As she waited for the water to boil, she opened the freezer compartment of the refrigerator and looked at the assortment of TV dinners at her disposal.

Deciding on lasagna, she popped the foil-wrapped container into the oven, then turned and reached for a mug. She added a tea bag, hot water, then sat down at the table, idly stirring the hot liquid as she contemplated the lonely evening ahead.

It was one of many she'd spent since returning to New Orleans. It wasn't that she lacked the opportunity, but it boiled down to the fact that she simply wasn't interested in going out, at least to the extent most of her friends, and especially Claire and Jacques, thought she should be.

Strangely enough, her brother and his wife never mentioned Greg. Claire knew the story, of course, and had been a tremendous comfort at the time. Jacques had, however, by his very silence from the moment of her break with Greg, caused Sam to feel that he blamed her for the divorce. With a consideration that was normally lacking in their relationship, the brother and sister had drawn an unspoken truce where Greg was concerned. Sam asked no questions about her ex-husband . . . he volunteered no information.

The aroma of the lasagna prompted Sam to get to her feet. She took salad makings from the refrigerator and a half-loaf of French bread. The bottle of wine she had chilling would add a festive touch to the meal, and hopefully lift her sagging spirits.

CHAPTER FIVE

Sam was just on the point of uncorking the bottle of wine when the sound of the doorbell broke the silence in the small house.

She closed her eyes, a resigned expression on her face at the untimely interruption. "Why now?" she murmured, stalking out of the kitchen and down the hall, the bottle of wine, the corkscrew halfway into the cork, clutched to her chest.

There was a decidedly cross look on her face as she opened the door. But instead of a neighbor or a salesman as she'd expected, she found Greg.

"Hello," he drawled in an amused voice, his dark eyebrows raised comically at the lack of enthusiasm emanating from the lady of the house. "Perhaps I've called at a bad time?" He smiled as a tiny grin replaced Sam's frown.

"Not at all," she replied, stepping aside so that he could come in. "I'd just gotten my dinner on the table," she explained, moving the wine bottle she was still clutching. "I thought you were a salesman or something."

"Perish the thought," Greg remarked dryly, making no attempt to enter the room. "Did you say you were about to have dinner?"

"Yes. Why?"

"You'll see," he threw over his shoulder, then turned and bounded down the walk toward his car. Sam stood in the doorway, feasting her eyes on him, uncaring that she was gawking like a teenager. For in spite of the warnings of the past she knew that the depression she'd felt earlier—when her plans for the evening had been called off—stemmed from the disappointment of knowing she wouldn't be seeing Greg. It did little for her self-esteem to admit that in only three short days he'd managed to turn her well-ordered life into an erratic sequence of unbelievable highs and lows, governed solely by his absences and appearances.

It was a more subdued Sam who watched Greg's progress back up the walk, his arms laden with a large box. Again she stepped aside to allow him into her home. You never once imagined that your reunion with Greg would go smoothly, her conscience insisted, so stop moaning . . . enjoy.

Greg turned, noting the change in her. "Something happened to upset you while I was out at the car?" His slightly mocking tone was not missed by Sam. He knew nothing had happened . . . It was simply his way of letting her know he was still capable of discerning her moods and that he was also aware of this latest change.

"No," Sam replied, meeting his mocking gaze with her equally level one. "Nothing that time won't take care of." She waved him toward the kitchen, following close behind.

Moments later the lonely serving of lasagna was put in the refrigerator and the white cartons of Chinese food were spread out—everything from shrimp with lobster sauce to three fortune cookies.

"Why three?" Sam asked taking down another plate from the cupboard over the sink.

"For Elizabeth, of course," Greg remarked shortly, as though all thirteen-month-old toddlers were anxiously awaiting such a treat. "How is she, by the way?" He heaped both plates with enormous helpings of everything in sight.

"Feeling miserable, poor little tyke. She has a red throat, swollen tonsils, and infected ears. It usually lasts only a couple of days, then she's back to normal."

"What do you normally do if she gets sick during the week? Do you still leave her with your neighbor?" he asked frowningly as he held one of the oak chairs for Sam and then took the one opposite.

"It depends. I trust Mrs. Gautier completely, and Claude's very understanding when it comes to my taking off from work."

"I'm sure he is," Greg growled. "Most men are very understanding when it comes to the woman in their life."

Sam shot him a deadly look. "Take your food and get the hell out of my house, Greg," she demanded, her chest heaving with anger. How dare he come into her own home and drop insulting remarks at will?

Her green eyes were snapping fire as she glared at him across the width of the table.

"Eat your dinner, Samantha. I happen to know how fond you are of Chinese food." His voice was infuriatingly calm. "If my casual references to Claude annoy you, my dear, then consider how I felt when I learned you were having an affair with that effeminate bastard."

"Damn you, Greg Howland!" she cried, coming to her feet in a burst of rage that caused her chair to topple backward and hit the floor. She braced her fists against the table, her slender frame leaning toward him. "For the last and final time, you narrow-minded jackass, I am not Claude Favret's woman! Nor have I ever exchanged anything so much as a simple peck on the cheek with him."

Her face was drained of color, her eyes brimming with the brillance of unshed tears. "I'm sick of defending myself against a pack of lies told to you by that jealous bitch, Monica. Yes," she rushed on in a furious spate, seeing Greg's eyes narrow at the mention of his secretary's name. "I found out only yesterday that I have her to thank for your low opinion of me. However, considering the source of your information, it's occurred to me that your love couldn't have been all it was cracked up to be or you would have had more faith in me."

At the conclusion of her outburst Sam turned away from him and walked over to the counter, willing herself to get a grip on her emotions. She hated herself for being so weak as to allow Greg's baiting to get to her. But his constant chipping away at her had driven her beyond the bounds of self-control, caused her to lash out in retaliation for what she knew to have been a premeditated attack on her character.

Suddenly Sam sensed him behind her, the heat from his body passing through to her skin and warming her with its intensity. "Look at me, Samantha," he commanded, his voice husky. His touch on her arm was gentle as he turned her around to face him. "What I'm about to say seems to have all the earmarks of becoming a habit." A sad flicker briefly surfaced in his narrowed gaze before being absorbed in the sea-green depths. "But I am sorry. I didn't come here to take cheap shots at you. Can you believe that?"

"I'd like to, Greg, I really would. But can you control your thoughts? The occasional cutting remarks that slip so easily from your lips?"

"I'm willing to try." His long arms slowly inched their way around her waist, his thighs pressing against her hips in a simple gesture that caused Sam's blood to run hot in her veins. "Are you?"

"I . . . I suppose so," she stammered, finding it difficult to think with his arms around her, his body pressing her backward against the rounded edge of the counter. "I'd like for us to be friends."

"We'll never be friends, Samantha." Greg released a ragged sigh. "Ours is destined to be a love-hate relationship, and you damn well know it."

Sam wanted to argue, to point out that it was his jealousy that was responsible for the seemingly un-bridgeable gap that existed between them . . . that and Monica's lies. Then she paused. No, she remind-ed herself as she returned his tortured gaze, I can't accept that. Some way, somehow I'll prove to you that you're wrong about me.

"Perhaps," she said with deliberate coolness, a state she was far from feeling at the moment. "But right now I think I'd settle for your friendship."

Greg tilted his head to one side and looked at her for several mind-tingling seconds. Slowly a smile broke the sensuous curve of his lips, bringing a wealth of memories flooding into Sam's mind. She'd seen that smile on his face in times past when she'd done or said something that particularly amused him.

"Funny . . . but by now I'd have thought you'd have lost it."

"What?"

"That innate ability you have of looking at the world through rose-colored glasses." He allowed one hand to ease upward over her back and shoulders, his fingers trailing softly against the skin of her neck, and finally the gentle cupping of her cheek. His thumb lightly caressed the outline of her slightly pouting lips. "I'm not so sure about this 'friendship' you seem to be so keen on, baby, but I sure as hell know that I have to keep on seeing you."

Sam wasn't sure who moved first, nor did she really care. She was aware only of Greg's lips capturing hers in a kiss that was a combination of desire, savagery, and a hint of cruelty. He gave no mercy in his relentless quest, and Sam asked for none.

With each searching thrust of his tongue, she met, teased, and withdrew with her own, not caring that she was opening a door that couldn't be closed again. It was as though the hands of time had been rolled back and there was only she and Greg, their desire for each other a wild and exciting spiral that danced and swirled on its ever-moving upward journey.

The touch of hands . . . warm and familiar on her breasts, had Sam arching her back like a taut bowstring, shamelessly seeking the touch, urging him to continue with the sensually exciting movement of her body against his.

Suddenly he drew back, his breath escaping in labored gasps. "This isn't enough, baby." His emerald gaze bored into her dulled one. "I need you, have to have you."

Sam felt the sinewy strength of an arm slip under her knees, another around her shoulders, and found herself being swept up against a chest as hard as stone. "Will you let me make love to you?" Greg whispered, his head lowering as his lips nibbled at the swollen softness of hers, his tongue tracing their fullness in an erotic gesture that had Sam shuddering with anticipation.

"Yes . . ." she whispered throatily, never once thinking of denying him.

Greg strode from the kitchen and into Sam's bedroom. Their gazes met and held as he allowed her to slip slowly from his arms, her body in full contact with the warmth of his. Her breasts tightened excitedly, the sensitive tips engorging themselves, meshing with the solidity of his chest as she slid down the length of him.

She lifted trembling hands to the front of the dark blue shirt, her fingers at first stumbling as she released one button, growing steadier with the next . . . and the next, until she had found her way to the coarse mat of dark hair on his bronze chest. Her touch became bolder, the tips of her fingers stealing in and out of the short, curly hair, lightly brushing the tiny nipples she found nestling in the thick growth.

Surprised and at the same time pleased by her boldness, Greg found his resolve to move slowly fast deserting him. He gave a hoarse groan from deep inside his throat, his hands caught the edge of the cotton shirt and drew it upward, over her head.

There was the briefest of pauses as his eyes took in the rounded loveliness of the small, firm breasts, their turgid points posed in readiness for his touch.

"God!" he murmured brokenly, "but you're more lovely than I remembered." He bent his head until his lips closed over one enticing morsel and then the other.

When his hands inserted themselves between their bodies and tugged at the fastening of the denims Sam was wearing, she instinctively widened the gap, allowing him complete freedom. She felt the downward thrust of the zipper, then his hands . . . warm and caressing as they slipped beneath the bikini briefs and clutched her buttocks in a firm grasp, pressing her against the heated arousal of his body.

Of their own accord both bodies sought the softness of the bed; the silken refuge of the blue coverlet was cooling to their heated flesh. Sam closed her eyes against the merciless waves of passion that were sweeping over her, the sound of her pounding heart.

In the midst of this crescendo she felt Greg pulling back from her. Through slitted eyes glittering with desire and longing, she saw him braced above her, his huge fists supporting his upper body, his head tilted to one side.

"Greg?" she protested feebly, reaching up and clasping his neck with one slim hand.

"Shhhh," he murmured softly, pushing away and rising to his feet. "I hear Elizabeth, honey." He quickly tucked the tail of his shirt back into his jeans and buttoned up the front.

"Elizabeth!" Sam cried out, crashing back to earth with a resounding thud. She scrambled from the bed and started toward the door.

"Hold it." Greg stopped her with a strong hand on her arm. "I'll go to her. You put your shirt on."

Sam looked down in mortified confusion at her nakedness. "Th . . . thank you," she whispered, then began pulling her clothes back on.

By the time she was dressed and hurrying toward Elizabeth's room, she'd made very little headway in calming her screaming nerves. It was as though each nerve ending was frayed, and the only sovereign remedy being Greg's hands, his lips, his body moving against hers with compelling force. She'd always known their relationship had been explosive, but being without him for three years had created a smoldering fire inside Sam that had startled her with its intensity.

Sooner or later there was bound to be a reckoning, just as there would have been only moments ago but for her daughter's interruption.

The sight that greeted Sam as she entered Elizabeth's room blocked all thoughts of desire from her mind. She saw Greg sitting on the edge of the bed, calmly soothing the fretful little girl, his large hands stroking her small body. "Did she . . . Oh, no," Sam wailed, a sour odor pricking at her nostrils. She looked at the bed and saw the evidence. "Oh, dear," she muttered. "Could you . . . I hate to ask, but would—"

"Why don't you take Elizabeth into the bathroom and clean her up while I take care of the bed?" Greg interrupted in a matter-of-fact way. He looked down at the little girl on his lap, the fever raging in her small body adding an unusually rosy glow to her tiny cheeks. "It's all right, sweetheart. You go with Mommy, and I'll be right here when you get back, okay?" He seemed oblivious to the state of his expensive shirt, which bore the marks of Elizabeth's recent accident. In fact, his whole manner quite astounded Sam.

The next few minutes were hectic ones as far as Elizabeth was concerned. Her usual sunny disposition was overshadowed by her illness, leaving her cranky and fussy as Sam bathed her.

During the general confusion in the bathroom, with Sam's continued gentle bathing of her daughter and Elizabeth's howls of indignation at such unnecessary tomfoolery, Greg walked in.

Immediately Elizabeth turned her biggest guns of persuasion on this huge person in whom she'd found a very accommodating friend. She looked up at him with tears glimmering in the green brightness of her eyes, her tiny chin quivering pitifully. Two chubby arms reached for him.

Sam's reaction to this display of feminine wiles fell

halfway between amusement and irritation. "Don't be taken by her pathetic helplessness," she cautioned Greg, who had squatting down beside the tub, a stricken look on his rugged face. "She's the biggest flirt I've ever seen. Add to that being spoiled, and you have quite a combination."

"That's not so at all, is it, Elizabeth?" he murmured to the unhappy toddler. "You're very discerning in your choice of friends, aren't you, princess?"

Before Sam could reach for the large towel she'd placed on the dressing table, Greg already had it and was lifting Elizabeth from the tub. He wrapped her snugly in the voluptuous folds, murmuring consolingly as he carried her back to her room.

Sam followed, her brows arching in surprise at the crisply made bed, the sheets neatly tucked, as tight as if she'd done the job herself.

"Let's get her into her pajamas, and then I'll rock her to sleep," Greg informed Sam in a manner that bespoke complete competence where small children were concerned.

"Oh?" she asked perversely as she hurried over to the narrow chest and got out clean sleeping gear. "And what do you plan on rocking her in?" Her personal relationship with him was one thing, but to deliberately attempt to take control of her daughter was another matter.

"You mean to tell me you don't own a rocking chair?" His expression of shock caused Sam's lips to twitch upward in spite of her annoyance.

"No," she pointedly replied. "Does that make me some kind of monster?"

"Don't be ridiculous, Samantha. But the fact remains that all babies should be rocked. It's . . . it's unfeeling not to."

"Well, move over, Dr. Spock. You're about to be replaced by Greg Howland, noted . . . engineer!" she exclaimed acidly, taking Elizabeth away from him and laying her on the bed, where she dried, powdered, and dressed her.

"Honestly, you're as silly as Jacques. He'd like to see me married tomorrow so that Elizabeth would have a father. You carry on like a lunatic over the fact that she hasn't gotten motion sickness from being rocked to death! In case it's escaped your attention, my daughter and I have done quite well without you *or* Jacques." She glared at him through the cloud of baby powder, then promptly sneezed.

"And just who has your brother picked out as a suitable husband for you, Samantha?" Greg asked frostily, an angry pallor creeping over the tanned planes of his face.

"How the hell do I know?" she lashed out unthinkingly.

"Watch your language in front of the baby," he commanded, sounding for all the world like a first-class nerd!

Instead of flinging back a sharp retort, she merely glared at him. She settled Elizabeth in her bed, then

91

looked questioningly at him. "Would you mind watching her while I get her medicine?"

As she poured juice into a small glass and took the medicine from the refrigerator, Sam wondered at her peevishness toward Greg. For in all fairness, discounting his snide remarks about Claude, she'd enjoyed his company. In fact, there were moments when she'd let herself believe that he was Elizabeth's father and that the three of them were a normal, happy family.

Which is extremely risky, my dear, she remarked to herself. Because where you're seeing your reunion with Greg as a chance to prove you're not a two-timing hussy, you've no idea at all what his reasons are for seeing you.

Surely, she reasoned as she left the kitchen, there's some feeling left for me. Otherwise why put us both through senseless torment? It was a question that weighed heavily on her mind.

Once Elizabeth was settled, Sam found herself in the unique position of feeling embarrassed in Greg's presence. It was disconcerting, and she had no idea how to handle it.

Greg, completely at ease and vastly amused by her nervousness, took pity on her. "Shall we finish our dinner?" He offered his arm in a humorous gesture of gallantry.

Staring at him across the width of Elizabeth's cheery blue-and-white room, Sam could barely make out his dark features. She did, however, catch a flash of white as he smiled, dispelling the tension that had suddenly loomed between them.

"I think that's a terrific idea." Her answer was soft and warm; she was grateful that he'd refrained from calling attention to her discomfiture.

"But only if you'll remove your shirt," she added, laughing when his dark brows arched significantly. "I'm afraid my daughter has left us both rather smelly."

"Heavens, Samantha. For one wild, exciting moment I thought you were going to seduce me."

Sam gave him a measured look as she came forward and reached for the blue shirt he was shrugging out of. "Who knows? One day I may do just that. But I'm afraid tonight is out of the question. My daughter saw to that."

"And I thought she adored me." Greg sighed.

"You poor dear. Outsmarted by a baby. Can your ego stand the rejection?" she teased.

"By whom? Elizabeth or her mother?" he asked, smiling down at her.

Sam blushed furiously. She grabbed the shirt and fled, Greg's amused laughter floating after her.

CHAPTER SIX

Barely warm Chinese food had never tasted so good, Sam silently mused as she sat across from Greg, the sound of his deep voice lulling her into a state of contentment that brought a rosy glow to her cheeks.

The acute embarrassment she'd felt after their heated physical encounter had slowly dissipated as Greg skillfully steered the conversation to topics of innocuous generality.

His behavior was beyond reproach. It also brought a stirring of hope within Sam. She knew he wasn't in the least hesitant about showing his disdain for anyone or anything, leaving her to conclude that she wasn't the only one to feel the emotional pull between them. Whatever the reason, she was pleased. It brought her closer to her ultimate goal of proving her innocence, and hopefully having another chance with Greg.

"Did you have plans for your addition drawn up by an architect?" Greg asked, breaking into her pleasant reverie.

"Mmmm," Sam nodded, swallowing the sip of wine she'd just taken. She touched her napkin to her lips. "Would you like to see them?"

"Please."

Sam got up and walked over to the old-fashioned kitchen safe she treasured above all her many finds and opened a drawer. The plans were rolled up with a rubber band around them. She removed them and brought them back to Greg. "As you'll see, there's still quite a lot to be done." She cleared a space on the table so that he could lay out the blueprints.

It was difficult concentrating on the subject of renovations with the breadth of his bare shoulders so invitingly close. Sam drew a deep breath of determination, her eyes glued to the architect's drawings.

Greg studied the plans, one long forefinger going over each step. "Ah . . . that explains it," he mused, tapping the location of the wrought-iron staircase.

"What?" she asked curiously

"I wondered what on earth would possess you to put a stairway in your bedroom."

Sam laughed. "I suppose it does look out of place. But I had to go ahead and let them make the cut when I added the camelback. Otherwise, access to the upstairs would have been very limited."

"So . . . all that remains is to knock out that wall." He nodded toward the wall separating Sam's bedroom from the kitchen. "And the one in Elizabeth's room next to the living room. Right?"

"Almost," she answered, then explained. "Since these plans were drawn up I've decided to use the space that's now the closet in my bedroom . . . along with a small amount of space from this room to make a utility room. A place for my washer and dryer . . . a general catch-all."

"Sounds simple enough," Greg said. "Why don't you show me what you've got done to the upstairs?"

Sam hesitated. "It's . . . really a mess right now. Why don't you wait until I've finished it?"

He turned and looked at her, bringing his face excitingly close to her breasts. Before she could step back, a strong arm closed about her waist. "I'm an engineer, remember? Seeing things in a state of confusion is hardly new to me."

"Okay," she reluctantly agreed, "but as you should remember, I'm not very organized."

"It's not your organization nor your tidiness that interests me, Samantha," he countered smoothly, drawing her between his legs, his strong thighs and the arm at her waist holding her a willing captive.

There was a long, thoughtful silence between them as they stared at each other, each in his own way reliving the past and anxious to get on with the mystery the future held.

"It's still there, baby," Greg rasped huskily, his

96

hands settling on the slender curves of her buttocks, forcing her breasts into direct contact with his mouth.

Sam raised trembling hands to the dark head, molding her fingers to the curve of his skull and absorbing the pivotal thrust as his lips tugged at first one firm nipple and then the other.

In a gesture of surrender that didn't go unnoticed by Greg, Sam let her hands slide down either side of the thick column of his neck and come to rest on his shoulders. With gentle, infinitely tender movements of her long, slim fingers, she began to message the tanned skin, feeling the involuntary flexing of the powerful muscles as she continued the soothing motion.

Oh, God! How she wanted him. Wanted the sameness of a day-to-day relationship with him. She was the addict . . . he, her fix.

Her eyes were closed against the quivering warmth, the moist desire that quickened that innermost softness of her being. Her legs became rubbery, depending on the sinewy strength of Greg's thighs to keep her upright. The small sigh of pleasure that escaped her lips drew an answering groan from Greg. His mouth ceased its quest as his face nuzzled the fullness beneath the thin material of her shirt.

With a sudden thrust Greg pushed Sam back and stood upright, his strong hands steadying her. She opened her eyes, their emerald brilliance clouded by desire. "This isn't the time, Samantha," he murmured hoarsely. "I want no interruptions, no ghosts haunting our lovemaking."

"Are you so certain we will make love?" she managed to croak, hoping to quash the hint of triumph, the assuredness in his voice, and failing miserably.

"Oh, yes, and so were you the minute we set eyes on each other in Antoine's. I'd go to hell and back to know the pleasure of making love to you again. Do you remember how it was, Samantha, the way you clung to me, crying out my name?"

Even in her muddled state, bemused by the memories his words were forcing her to relive, Sam detected the subtle edge of revenge, the desire to hurt that had insinuated itself into the midst of their explosive union.

"I remember, Greg," she whispered, meeting his gaze and holding it. "I also remember that you never used to want to hurt me."

"Nor do I now," he assured her, his speech clipped. "But when I think of you and that simpering bastard Favret, I could wring that beautiful neck of yours. It's eaten away at me for three agonizing years." His mouth curved into a harsh caricature of a smile. "I've spent endless nights undergoing the torments of a hell that no man should have to endure. It was always the same, with me being forced to watch that son-of-a-bitch caressing your lovely body, see him carrying you to the pinnacle of desire." His hands closed over the fragile bones of her shoulders. "Can you possible imagine being subjected to such a nightmare night after night?" His grip bit into her skin like hot fetters of steel.

"You still won't believe me, will you?" Sam cried out. The physical pain he had inflicted was nothing compared to the pain ripping her heart. "How could you possibly have believed such a filthy lie about me, when you knew Monica had been chasing you for years? She'd have done anything . . . and did . . . to discredit me in your eyes."

For a moment was there the tiniest flicker of hope, . . . unease, in the depths of his gaze, only to be masked just as quickly? "Are you still sticking to that ridiculous story, that Favret was sick and that you only stopped by his place to keep him abreast of what was going on at the office? That your staying overnight with him was nothing more than a charitable gesture on your part?"

"Yes, Greg, I am. It's not a story, it's the truth," she replied as calmly as possible. "And some way I'll prove it."

"Why bother?" he questioned silkily, his fingers beginning to massage the skin he'd handled so carelessly only moments before. "Why is it so important, Samantha?"

She dropped her gaze, finding the crisp hair covering his chest to be just as disturbing. Space . . . she thought wildly . . . I have to put some space between us. She stepped around his intimidating hulk and began stacking the dishes they'd used. "Try putting yourself in my place, Greg. You've lived these past three years damning my soul to hell, hating me for my supposed infidelity. Well, let me tell you, sweetie, it hasn't exactly been a picnic for me, either."

There was a grimly determined set to her small chin as Sam moved from table to sink, stubbornly refusing to look him in the face. She knew how likely it was they'd be sidetracked if she did, and it was vitally important that he know he wasn't the only one to have suffered from the nightmare that had driven them apart.

"I was humiliated and embarrassed by the story. Even my own brother still believes the worst about me. One minute I was happy beyond all belief . . . madly in love with my husband and he with me . . . or so I thought. The next thing I knew, he was standing in front of me like some grim executioner, accusing me of being unfaithful to him, refusing to listen to a single word I said." At that moment she did face him, turning away from the sink, her hands gripping the edge. "I had nightmares as well, Greg, nightmares that tore at me until I was sure I would go crazy. Fortunately I met John."

Her eyes softened as the memory of John's kindness, his infinite gentleness, swept over her. "I told him my story, Greg, holding nothing back. Do you know what he did? He laughed at your stupidity. And then he took me inside that inexplicable aura of compassion he possessed, his love and faith like a blaze of sunshine. One of my deepest regrets is that

he never lived to see Elizabeth. Somehow I'd felt
. . . hoped that giving him a child would repay him
in a small way for his trust at a time in my life when
I needed it so desperately."

When she finished speaking, a pregnant silence
hovered over them, stretching into an uncomfortable
length of time. Greg stood motionless, his granite
features rigid, his eyes like chips of ice. Sam lowered
her head, reached for a dishcloth, and drew it back
and forth over her trembling hands.

The closeness, the intimacy they'd shared before
Greg's outburst was gone, leaving the gulf between
them deeper than ever, the two of them staring at
each other across the bottomless abyss. Pain, distrust, confusion, even anger echoed in the cavernous
depths, with no possible bridge to span the yawning
darkness.

When Sam thought she couldn't bear this horrible
waiting another minute, Greg moved. He picked up
his shirt, then turned and walked to the kitchen door.
There he paused, his large hands splayed in a bracing
stance on either side of the frame, his head bowed.
"I'll call you later, Samantha. Right now I need to
be alone."

She took a tentative step forward, a hand out-
stretched toward him. "Greg. . . . can't we? . . ."

"Later, Samantha, later," he murmured, staying
her progress with one hand thrown up in a gesture
of defense.

Sam stood frozen, her eyes on his retreating back

as he strode down the hall and out the front door. She watched him go with a resurgence of all the old hurts, the same empty feeling of utter desolation settling over her.

She slowly turned back to the cluttered kitchen, her eyes unseeing as she stumbled toward the table and dropped wearily into a chair. Oh, God! she cried out in silent supplication. I did so want him to believe me.

The horrible tightness in her chest threatened to impede her breathing as she gave in to the overwhelming desolation. She was beginning to have an awesome sense of déjà vu, and Sam wasn't sure she could survive this second time around.

Greg had been correct in his assertion that a confrontation between them was inevitable. Sam had known this even before leaving Dallas. If it hadn't happened the way it did, she would have gone to see him. The expectation that he would believe her and sweep her up in his arms had become so fixed in her mind, she was now reeling from the shock of having that dream crumble at her feet.

"No!" she cried out, her eyes tightly closed as two small fists pounded the solid surface of the oak table, "Oh, no, please!" But the certainty wouldn't be denied. Her love for Greg Howland was as wasted as a drop of moisture on the parched sands of the desert.

In retrospect Sam could see how Monica's lies had shattered Greg; his jealousy dominated his nature to such an extent that he'd recoiled from Sam in horror. Now he was an embittered man, held captive by his pride, his ego. A prisoner whose only reprieve was in his own hands, in his ability to correctly distinguish truth from deceit . . . love from betrayal.

There was a sluggishness to her movements as she eventually forced herself to get up. Practicality took over by gently prodding her to return the kitchen to its original state of orderliness. In an almost drugged stupor she completed the chore, flipped the light switch off, and left the darkened room.

After checking on Elizabeth and pulling the covers back over the sleeping child, Sam entered the bathroom. She stripped, adjusted the water to the desired temperature, then stepped under the rushing torrent of water.

She closed her eyes and lifted her face to the soothing cascade that flowed over her, giving in to the relaxing sensation that invaded her senses from the warmth surrounding her. For several minutes she lingered in that ancient worshipful position, letting the water act as a catharsis. Relieving her, if only temporarily, of the burdensome weight of depression that bore down on her slim shoulders.

Necessity, in the shape of her daughter's cherubic face, drew Sam back to the realm of reality and its unpleasantness. She turned off the water, pushed back the shower door, and reached for the towel.

But it wasn't the towel her hand encountered. Instead, she touched a hard, muscled thigh, the feel of sturdy material beneath her fingertips.

Sam froze in this bent position, her other hand quickly raking back the strands of wet hair and the water streaming down her face. When she opened her eyes, they slid over her hand . . . still frozen against the denim-clad leg.

She willed her gaze to move upwards to the partially exposed chest, the clefts on either side of the strong-columned neck where the thrust of the collarbone could be seen. The fear that had held her in the paralyzed grip of panic subsided. There was disbelief in her eyes as she slowly straightened up.

"Why?" she finally asked in a faint whisper. "Why did you come back?"

"I had to," Greg stated simply. "I got as far as the end of the block, but I couldn't go any farther. I've been sitting outside in my car, trying to get up enough courage to come back in."

"Courage? You, Greg? When have you ever lacked courage?" Sam asked sadly. Suddenly she became aware of her nakedness, of the warmth of Greg's gaze as it lingered on the slim length of a shapely thigh merging with a taut, flat stomach, tapering into a slim waist.

She made a move for the towel which had fallen to the ceramic-tiled floor, only to have Greg stop her. His hand caught hers, drawing her inexorably toward him. "I want you, Samantha," he murmured. "God help me, but I can't get you out of my mind."

"I know," she breathed the words, following the irresistible pull of his hand until they stood toe to toe. Instead of feeling shame, Sam held herself proudly, her face framed by already curling tendrils of dark hair.

Slowly, as if they were actors in a play, Greg drew her fully against him, his lips voraciously devouring hers as both gave in to the raging inferno that was now beyond all control.

Sam could feel the hard drumming of Greg's heart against her breasts as his hands ran feverishly from her shoulders to buttocks in his effort to completely consume her with his being.

"Ah . . . this is so good, Samantha," he rasped against her ear. "I've almost died for the smell of you, the taste of your body." He eased her back away from him so that he could look into her eyes.

With her own emerald eyes aglow with the flame of anticipation, Sam slowly raised her hands upward to the front of his shirt and began unbuttoning it. When his chest was bared, she pushed the garment from his shoulders, a slight movement from Greg allowed the soft material to slide down over his arms and hands to the floor.

Instead of hurrying the process, Sam savored each tantalizing moment as she caressed the bronze skin with her eyes and her hands. A tiny quiver coursed down her spine as her fingers roamed the wiry covering beneath her touch, as each familiar spot of arousal was sought out.

She stood on tiptoe and touched the tip of her hot, moist tongue to the wildly beating pulse in Greg's neck, letting her lips burn a fiery path downward to his waist.

Impatient with the barrier she encountered, Sam tugged awkwardly at the stubborn metal fastener of his jeans. Her body was on fire for the release that only he could give her, her thoughts overrun by exquisite memories of being held in his arms as they rode the tide of passion.

With an adroitness that barely penetrated the cloak of ecstasy surrounding them, Greg dealt with his remaining clothes. When he swept Sam up against his chest, she encircled his neck with her arms, gasping aloud and closing her eyes at the exciting friction between the crisp growth of hair on his chest and the painfully sensitive tips of her breasts.

But instead of moving toward the bedroom, Sam felt the momentary brush of cold metal against her arm. Her eyes flew open in astonishment as she felt herself being lowered, her feet coming to rest on the floor of the shower.

"What? . . ." she murmured in shocked protest, her look of incredulity encountering the dancing twinkle in Greg's eyes as he leaned forward and turned on the water, then adjusted the spray.

"Don't tell me you've forgotten," he said accusingly, reaching for the fragrant soap. He worked the perfumed bar between his brown palms till a mass of frothy bubbles covered both hands.

"No." Sam smiled slowly, the wealth of love in her heart reflected in her face. "You quite ruined me where showers are concerned," she huskily replied, their gazes holding amid the electric storm of emotion permeating the confined space.

The memory of his deft, deliberate touch had somehow diminished among the myriad remembered pleasures in her mind, and Sam gave in to the hands that began caressing her body with the expertise of a masseur. Every inch of her was subjected to the arousing ministrations of his hands, steadily fueling the fire that was building within her.

When Greg turned her around, so that her back was to him, her hips resting against his thighs, her back and shoulders fitting against the taut, flat stomach and broad chest, Sam knew she was at the end of her endurance. In further affirmation of the overwhelming force driving her, she caught Greg's hand that was resting on the curve of her waist and lifted it to her face. She pressed her lips to his palm, then guided it to the frantic throbbing of her heart.

"Greg, I need you . . ."

At the sound of her voice, the desperate entreaty he heard, Greg helped the flow of water in rinsing off the remaining suds by briskly running his hands from her shoulders to buttocks, then from breast to thigh.

Once the water was turned off, Sam found her body being wrapped in the thick folds of a towel. The next moment, she was caught up in Greg's arms and carried to the bedroom and the blue-satin—covered bed.

There was an unrestrained tangle of limbs as they sought the softness of the bed, which Greg quickly set to rights by turning Sam onto her back as he knelt beside her. The dim light from the window cast a luminous glow over the magnolia creaminess of Sam's body. Greg stared at her with worshipful wonder, almost afraid that if he blinked his eyes, she would disappear.

It was Sam who broke the spell by touching his thigh and letting her fingertips dance ever so lightly in an ever-widening circle that soon had Greg shuddering beneath her onslaught.

He eased the length of his body alongside Sam's. She was watching him . . . wanting him, the hunger glowing in the emerald depths of her eyes. His eyes narrowed at the sight of the open invitation so clearly beckoning him.

He lowered his head and teased one throbbing nipple with the hot tip of his tongue. At her indrawn gasp of pleasure, Greg took the taut tip in his mouth and gently sucked, drawing an essence from her that was more intoxicating than the finest wine.

His hands roamed the familiar curves and plains, knowing the precise hidden spots that would coax pleasurable moans from her parted lips. His hand kneaded her stomach, then slipped down to caress the silken length of her slim thighs.

"Oh, Greg," Sam groaned, her hips arching

against his hand, shamelessly begging for a further invasion of the center of her desire.

"Samantha," Greg growled as his lips followed the path blazed by his hands. "I've been dreaming of this moment for three years," he moaned, his voice gravelly with emotion.

In response Sam reached for him, one hand cupping his neck and drawing his lips to her own. The kiss they shared was a simple merging of their separate desires into one . . . shutting out all thoughts of doubt and blame.

When Greg sought the softness of her inner thighs, they opened like a dew-kissed bud at the slightest touch of his leg against hers. His entry into the burning center of her brought a strangled cry of release from Sam's lips. . . . She was whole again.

CHAPTER SEVEN

Sam was curled in the cozy comfort of Greg's arms, her head resting on his shoulder. There was a lethargic droop to the hand that idly threaded its fingers through the dark hair that covered his chest. Their lovemaking had been charged with an urgency that had left them both sated.

Greg had loved her in every way imaginable, carrying her to the summit time and time again. Sam eventually lost count as time hung suspended, and only his hands, his body, molding her . . . shaping her to his thrusting rhythm, held any meaning.

She refused to give in to her thoughts of tomorrow, reveling in each exciting moment of his nearness. Tomorrow would have to take care of itself.

Greg suddenly stilled the fingers that had found

and were teasing the nipples in the wiry growth on his chest, brought them to his lips, and kissed them, one by one. "Are you happy, baby?" The whispered question stirred the soft hair against her temple.

"Oh, yes," Sam confessed. "In fact, I can't think of a nicer way to become exhausted." She snuggled closer, if possible, to his warmth. She moved one foot against a tanned leg, her toes gliding over the hair-roughened skin in a teasing game of enticement.

"No, you don't," he growled, making a grab for her leg. "Don't move another inch, or I won't be held responsible."

"Why, Greg," she said coyly. "Have I exhausted you already?"

"No, you insatiable little baggage, and you know it. We've plenty of time for this sport of kings. Any further overtures from you would blow my mind, and I want to talk to you." He released her leg and playfully slapped her on her bare bottom.

"Well," Sam snorted in feigned annoyance, flouncing over to her side of the bed and glaring at the ceiling. "I can tell when I'm not wanted."

"Really?" Greg grinned indulgently, turning over onto his side and observing her display of pique. "Our activities for the last few hours don't count, hmmmm?"

"Oh, that"—she waved one small hand dismissively—"a mere trifle, my man, a mere trifle," she remarked, calling on all her self-control to keep from laughing as his features contorted into a hideous grimace.

"I'll trifle with you some," he growled menacingly, then pounced on her, hauling her on top of his chest and holding her there with both arms. "Now, Samantha, let's hear more." One large hand snaked down and caressed the softness of her buttocks. "I'd say you are in rather a vulnerable position at the moment to do a lot of complaining, wouldn't you?"

"Only a heartless brute would threaten a woman he's just made love to." Sam spoke without conviction, finding the position infinitely pleasing.

"God!" Greg muttered, his hands clutching her to him convulsively. "I can't get enough of you."

"I know . . . I know," Sam whispered, drunk with the realization of the power she held over him. But instead of him loving her again as she'd hoped, Greg surprised her by easing her off him and jackknifing into a sitting position, his shoulders resting against the walnut headboard, his smoldering gaze passing over each delectable inch of her.

Sam watched this possessive appraisal of her body with fascinated pride. She knew that look of old . . . and it intrigued her, adding untold confidence to her campaign of regaining Greg's love and trust.

"You're a shameless baggage, Samantha Howland," he said, dropping one large hand to the curve of her hip.

Sam showed a flicker of surprised satisfaction at his slip of the tongue, but decided against pointing out his little faux pas. It pleased her that Greg was also shackled by the memories of the past. "I do aim to please, sir," she answered in the same teasing vein as before.

"Ahh . . . you do, and quite well. In some respects, that is," he remarked dryly, a frown drawing the dark brows together in a stern line.

"What are you talking about?" Sam asked, puzzled.

"Has it occurred to you to wonder how I got back into your house?"

"No . . . I just assumed . . . that is, I . . ." she shook her head, a frown marring her brow. "How did you get in?"

"Quite simple, actually. I jimmied your lock."

"But I didn't hear you!" she exclaimed.

"You were in the shower, Samantha, remember? I went through the house at a leisurely pace, checking on Elizabeth, the windows and the other door," he grimly informed her.

"My God!" She rolled over on her back, a shaft of fear hitting her. "That's frightening."

"I meant it to be. Do you realize I could have been a burglar with easy access to you and your daughter?"

"Okay, okay. I get your point. You don't have to scare me to death," Sam retorted, not wanting to hear any more grim predictions. "I'll have new locks installed in the morning."

"*I'll* have new locks installed," Greg corrected

113

her. "I don't want to have to hope you and Elizabeth are safe, I want to be certain you are."

"That's not nec—"

"Don't argue, Samantha," he demanded, raising a tanned finger to her lips to stop the flow of protest, and she didn't.

Nor did she the next morning, when at approximately nine thirty a man appeared on her doorstep in a gray uniform with the name of a reputable locksmith in neat letters above the left pocket of his shirt.

After assuring himself that Sam's was the proper address, he set to work installing not only the conventional lock Greg had jimmied, but a dead bolt as well. The back door received the same treatment, as did each of the windows, with a complicated contraption that proved almost impossible for Sam to work.

As the man was gathering up his tools in preparation for leaving, Sam got her checkbook from her purse. "How much do I owe you?"

"Not a thing. Mr. Howland took care of it, ma'am."

She didn't pursue the subject, merely smiled her thanks as she showed the man out. Once the door was closed however, the smile disappeared, replaced by a frown. She didn't want Greg paying for her locks.

Sam prided herself on supporting Elizabeth and herself. She knew part of her determination stemmed from a remark Jacques had made when she divorced

114

Greg and moved to Dallas. "You'll probably starve to death without Greg or me there to bail you out," he'd muttered disgustedly. Later Sam realized the statement had been made under duress. To her brother she was still his little sister, about as capable as a two-year-old of looking after herself. But the words had been tantamount to waving a red flag in front of her.

But lately, due to Elizabeth's unfortunate bouts with tonsillitis, the accompanying medical bills, and her own efforts to finish the renovation of her small house, Sam was beginning to feel decidedly cramped financially. No matter how closely she watched what she spent, there seemed to be a steadily declining balance in her bank account each month. And to add insult to financial injury, on this particular Saturday morning she knew she had to sit down and try to balance her checkbook and pay her bills.

A while later, after a quick job of cleaning, Sam sat down, fortified with a pot of strong coffee and with a cup of the aforementioned brew at hand, along with one of the cigarettes she smoked occasionally, she began the obnoxious chore. Her only pleasure as she labored were the comforting noises that came from Elizabeth, who was settled in her playpen in the middle of the kitchen floor. She just gotten the irritating mess sorted out and was beginning to add up her checks, when the doorbell sounded.

Sam cast a grim eye at her watch and rose to her

feet. She was still frowning when she opened the door.

"Good morning, Samantha," Greg said pleasantly, looking for all the world as though he'd had twelve hours of sleep, though Sam knew exactly what time he'd left her house. He was dressed in his favorite faded jeans, a pullover knit shirt in dark blue, and a Windbreaker of the same color as the shirt. Noticeably lacking were the lines of tension in his face that had been so obvious on his previous visits. "Aren't you going to ask me in?"

"Of course," she murmured, then stepped aside. How was she to act toward him? In spite of having been married twice, Sam found herself in somewhat of a quandary. Entertaining the man she'd let make love to her the night before was a first for her.

"Is something wrong?" Greg asked, unable to ignore her obvious agitation. "Is Elizabeth worse?"

"Oh, no . . . no. She's much better. Her temperature is almost back to normal." She eagerly latched onto the decoy . . . anything to escape Greg's eagle-sharp gaze. "We're in the kitchen." Sam smiled and started to walk past him.

"Just a minute, little one." He stopped her and turned her around to face him, his large, capable hands casually caressing her arms.

"Are you having second thoughts about last night?" There was a slight furrowing of the skin above the bridge of his nose as he tried to gauge her mood. "What's happened since I left here, Samantha?" His hands closed in a firm grip on each of her arms.

"Nothing's happened, Greg," Sam quickly assured him. She smiled. "I realize I'm not some virtuous maiden, but I also find I'm lacking in sophistication when it comes to the morning after."

Greg exhaled roughly, drawing Sam to him in an embrace that threatened to do permanent damage to her ribs. "God, Samantha, don't scare me like that again, hmmm?" he murmured against the softness of her dark hair. He caught her chin and tilted her face upward, his lips covering hers in a kiss that left no room for doubt.

His tongue sought the tender recesses of her mouth, then engaged her own pink tongue in a game of seduction that soon had Sam clinging to him for support, the pliant thrust of her slender body molding itself to his solid form.

When his mouth left the softness of her lips and sought the throbbing pulse at the side of her neck, Sam felt the tremor hit his body, heard the sharp intake of air into his lungs. "As far as sophistication goes, how do you think I feel? Two minutes with you and I'm trembling like some damn kid who's still wet behind the ears." He drew back and looked down into her face. "Suppose we take events as they come, and not worry about analyzing every little thing?"

"Sounds simple enough," Sam agreed huskily, even though her thoughts were at variance with the assuredness of her voice. There was no doubt she wanted him, but she had to have his trust as well. She knew she couldn't stand the uncertainty of a truce with Greg. "It's just that everything seems to be moving at such a frantic pace. I . . . I can't quite take it all in."

Greg caught her face between his palms, his green eyes blazing as he stared at her, his gaze compelling her to look at him. "I know there are questions in both our minds, baby, and a lot more. But we owe ourselves this time. The last three years have been hell for us both. Okay?"

Sam nodded, not feeling at all okay, but unable to say exactly why. There were so many conflicting emotions within her, too many to explain in a few minutes. Could she win his trust? She brushed aside the tiny fingers of doubt. She had no time for doubts . . . for negative thinking. All her energies must remain channeled into one Herculean task, and she refused to be distracted.

"Where's Elizabeth?" Greg's voice jerked her out of her tangled thoughts.

"In the kitchen. Would you care for a cup of coffee?"

"And some breakfast." He paused, a skeptical look skittering across his face. "Have you learned to cook?"

"No."

"Not even eggs?" he asked incredulously.

"A passable omelet. And I've learned not to scorch the bacon. Are you game?" The subject of her

118

culinary skills . . . or lack thereof . . . seemed to ease the tension of the moment.

Elizabeth spied Greg at once, and set up a pitiful howl, her chubby little arms reaching out to him. Greg removed his jacket, hung it on the back of a chair, and then picked up the little girl.

Sam watched out of the corner of her eye as she took eggs and bacon from the refrigerator. The sight of Greg taking to her daughter so quickly was rather puzzling. When she was married to him, Sam had brought up the subject of children many times, only to be told there was plenty of time. Privately she had concluded that jealousy played a major role in his decision. Greg had wanted his wife all to himself.

"What's this?" he asked, indicating the papers strewn all over the table. He pulled out a chair and sat down, his young admirer in his lap.

"My *bête noire*. I'm convinced the computer at the bank eats a sizable portion of my paycheck each month," she remarked acidly as she broke the eggs into a bowl.

"Are you having financial problems, Samantha?" Greg asked gruffly, picking up her statement and studying it without the slightest hesitation.

"Isn't everyone?"

Greg reserved comment. He finished his perusal of the statement and then thumbed through the canceled checks. "It seems to me that the princess has been ill more often than a child should be. What's the problem?"

"Tonsillitis," Sam answered.

"Then wouldn't it be simpler to have her tonsils out?"

"Nowadays doctors aren't so eager to perform surgery for any little illness. There's also a good chance Elizabeth will outgrow the problem, or so her pediatrician tells me."

"How did you manage to buy this house? Did Claude arrange it for you?" The resentment was still there, its edge a raw and ugly undercurrent. But in contrast to his earlier behavior, he waited for an answer to his question.

"No," Sam replied matter-of-factly, playing down the tense moment with deliberate casualness. "I used most of John's insurance money. To be quite honest, I didn't want anyone's help. I learned that with a child to raise, I didn't need to be dependent on anyone. Claude and Jacques were aghast that I bought this place without their approval."

She slid the bacon under the broiler, then looked over her shoulder at Greg. "Now you can understand why I'm so anxious to finish the renovations."

"Would you consider letting me help you?"

"Oh . . . I . . . no. I don't think so," Sam stuttered.

"Samantha . . ." The drawling pronunciation of her name signaled the annoyance her refusal had stirred up. "Don't you think you're being a bit ridiculous? We're not exactly strangers. After seeing the amount you've spent on medical bills for just one month"—he looked pointedly at the canceled checks —"I'd say you're fighting a losing battle."

"Perhaps," Sam muttered frowningly. "But I still can't accept your help, Greg. I do appreciate the offer, though."

"Three years have only served to increase your unbelievable stubbornness, Samantha," he growled. "However, if you won't accept my financial help, can you bring yourself to accept an offer of free labor?"

"Certainly. Another pair of hands is always welcome." She tilted the omelet pan, careful to keep the egg mixture from streaming down the outside of the pan, then poured Greg his promised cup of coffee. "As a matter of fact," she added, placing the mug of steaming coffee before him, "I'd planned on getting some work done this afternoon."

"What will we do with the princess?" he chuckled as Elizabeth, tired of being ignored, was reaching for everything within her grasp.

"You will carry her playpen upstairs, and," she said, eyeing him mischievously, "bring it back down when we're finished. For the moment, however, you may put her in her high chair. Your breakfast is ready."

Sam rested her head against the rounded lip of the tub and gave in to the soothing warmth of the water as it eased her aching muscles. Lord, but she was exhausted!

When she'd accepted Greg's offer, she had no idea

what she was letting herself in for. Not only did he work until after dark, but he'd enlisted Sean's help as well, and between the two of them, the house rang with the sound of hammering and sawing.

The last few pieces of the woven-textured paneling board was nailed in place, windows were faced, even the light fixtures were hung. Sam was demoted early in the proceedings to taking care of minor touchups with the paintbrush and seeing that a supply of cold beer was kept handy.

She couldn't help but smile as she remembered the look of surprise on Sean's face when he first arrived.

"What's up, Greg? You said something about helping Samantha? Are you two . . . I mean is? . . ." He floundered helplessly.

"Stop being so nosy, little brother," Greg growled. He caught Sean by the arm, pulled him inside, and closed the door. "This young lady is Elizabeth," he proudly proclaimed as though he alone were responsible for her being in the world.

Sean, captivated at once by Elizabeth's ready smile, held out his hands to her. Instead of falling into his arms as Sam assumed she would do, the teasing imp hid her small face in the curve of Greg's neck.

"Oh-ho . . ." Sean laughed. "Now I get the picture," he chuckled, ruffling the curls that capped Elizabeth's head. "Where's Sam?" he asked.

"Right here, Sean," Sam spoke up, smiling fondly at her former brother-in-law. She walked on into the room. "I hope you're ready to work. From the way that slave driver is talking," she said, nodding toward Greg, "I think we're in for a long day."

Later, when Greg grudgingly allowed them a break while he made some phone calls, Sean and Sam plopped down on the floor, leaning their weary backs against the wall.

"Samantha." Sean groaned miserably. "The next time you buy a house, please find one that isn't in need of a total overhaul. I've used muscles today I didn't even know I had," he complained.

"Direct all complaints to your dear brother, lazy-bones. He's the one who volunteered your services." She sighed. "I'd forgotten that he goes slightly bananas at the sight of a hammer and nails."

"I haven't," Sean growled. "Every damn place he's ever owned has been thoroughly worked over. I've threatened his life if he so much as moves a book in my apartment. By the way," he asked, slanting a questioning look toward her, "does this togetherness mean what I hope it does? Are the two of you getting back together?"

Sam gave him a halfhearted grin. "Who knows? There are still a lot of unanswered questions, a lot of doubt floating around. At least we've reached the point where we can talk without hurling insults at each other. Monica certainly did an excellent job of brainwashing Greg."

"Monica?" Sean asked, startled. "I know she was responsible for your original trouble, but I understood . . ." his voice trailed off. "Forget what I said. It's been a while, and I'm famous for getting things mixed up."

In a pig's eye! Sam thought meaningfully. Sean had a mind like a steel trap. He hadn't forgotten anything. More likely Greg had cautioned him against discussing Monica. The thought of that scheming hag being protected by Greg while Sam was thrown to the dogs was a bitter pill to swallow.

"Exactly where is Monica these days, Sean?"

"Houston."

"Houston? I'm surprised she would go that far from your brother. Everybody knew she'd been after him for years."

"Yes . . . well, I guess Greg got tired of her being constantly underfoot." He squirmed uncomfortably at Sam's continued pursuit of the subject.

"How long has she been in Houston?" Sam asked, refusing to let him off the hook so easily. His obvious discomfort was amusing, and she was inordinately curious about Monica's whereabouts.

"Going on three years," Sean replied, looking directly at her. "And I'm not answering any more questions, Miss Priss. Greg would have my head if he knew I'd talked as much as I have."

Sam shrugged, her mouth curving into a rueful moue. "It gets curiouser and curiouser. . . ." She favored him with a wicked grin.

At the end of the grueling day Greg suggested they go to his place for dinner. Sam declined the invitation, in spite of his frown of displeasure and the slight narrowing of his eyes. Her feigned headache wasn't entirely imaginary. The strain of the last few days and their whirlwind reunion had left her with an urge to be alone for a while.

She knew she wanted Greg back. That was a fact she'd accepted long ago. However, wanting him without having his trust wasn't to be considered. And at the moment Sam knew he was struggling with an enormous decision. And even though her love for him was a part of her that would never die, Sam also had her pride.

She wouldn't crawl, nor would she allow Greg to abuse her. Maturity, by way of her love for John and the birth of Elizabeth, had given Sam a new insight into Greg's complex personality. Jealousy was like a disease, and Greg was no exception. He had only one way of going at something . . . totally and completely. His belief that she'd been unfaithful to him had been pursued with that same singlemindedness, in all probability leaving him even more shattered than Sam.

When she made her decision to return to New Orleans, Sam recognized that proving her innocence would be a very iffy undertaking, but one she considered worth the effort. And even if it didn't result in their getting back together again, Sam felt she had to make the effort. The unfounded accusations had left deep emotional scars that only complete exoneration could heal.

CHAPTER EIGHT

Sunday passed in a flurry of activity for Sam. She was awakened at the unholy hour of six thirty by Greg, Sean, and two musclebound individuals who she later learned worked for Greg.

Sam stared in sleepy confusion at this army of masculinity that trooped into her tastefully decorated living room.

"Er . . . er . . . Greg?" she stammered, finally overcoming her initial shock and finding her voice. "Could I speak with you for a moment?"

"Go on into the kitchen and see if you think we should start there, Gus. I'll be with you in a second." Greg instructed the men. He turned to Sam, his gaze darkening perceptibly at the dewy freshness of her still sleep-warm face, the tousled condition of her

126

hair. The green robe, in a soft, clinging material, molded the outline of her slender figure.

He slowly closed the gap between them, his hands dropping to her waist and the beginnings of the gentle slope of her hips. "If you keep looking at me like that, Samantha, I'm afraid all the work on your house will come to a screeching halt," he growled, bending his head till his lips touched hers.

"Oh, really?" she teased, deliberately moving her hips against the hardness of his thighs, completely forgetting she'd wanted to question him closely about this invasion of her home on a Sunday morning. The power to excite him was exhilarating, leaving her slightly drunk with possibility.

"Samantha," Greg growled against her mouth, "behave before I embarrass us both." His strong white teeth sharply nipped the fullness of her bottom lip.

Sam absorbed the tiny prick of exquisite pain, the tip of her pink tongue caressing the spot, her eyes glowing with unrestrained desire. "Why, Greg," she purred, eyeing him provocatively from beneath thickly fringed lashes, "what a grouch you've become."

"You're very daring when you know you're safe." He frowned menacingly at her not-so-subtle attempts at seduction. "I'll remind you of your boldness when we're alone," he promised with a gleam of prospective retaliation in his eyes. "After you're dressed"—he let one finger trail lazily down the side of her throat and lower, to lose itself in the shadowy valley between her breasts—"how about making a pot of coffee? We'll send out for breakfast."

"Exactly what are you planning to do today?" she eventually got out, then frowned. "The walls? Are you going to knock out the downstairs walls?"

"You do want it done, don't you?" Greg mused, the corners of his eyes crinkling with amusement.

"Yes . . . but . . ."

"But . . . what?"

"My furniture . . . everything has to be moved, covered. There's also. . . . Oh, my gosh!" she exclaimed, a harassed expression clouding her face. "I talked with Jim last night and he's coming over after lunch to lay the upstairs carpet."

"So?" Greg asked, nonplussed. "Sounds to me like you're in business. Once the carpet's down, we can move your bedroom furniture upstairs. That'll leave only the work down here. Okay?"

"I suppose so," Sam answered faintly, feeling as though she'd been run over by a steamroller!

All the while she was dressing . . . in the privacy of the bathroom, the door securely locked . . . Sam could hear the activity of the men, the tentative tapping of a hammer and loud voices as they decided on just how to begin. She gritted her teeth and grimaced as she heard the unmistakable screech of a board being ripped from the wall. The monumental task awaiting her of transferring the bedrooms downstairs to the newly completed ones upstairs forced a groan of resignation from her.

She wondered—as she had so many times over the past week—at Greg's seemingly total absorption of her life, Elizabeth, and even her remodeling plans. There were also the explosive vibes that coursed between them each time they were together. Sam wasn't foolish enough to assume he'd forgotten the real reason for their divorce, nor his hatred for Claude. But there had been definite signs of thawing over the last couple of days, signs that gave her hope that another chance at happiness wasn't as far-fetched as she'd first imagined.

Mrs. Gautier, seeing the men coming in and out of the house and hearing the noise, came over to offer to help with Elizabeth. Sam introduced her neighbor to Greg, smiling at how easily he captured the petite matron's heart. By the time Sam had packed a small bag for her daughter, Mrs. Gautier was positively beaming with approval.

"He's such a charming man, Samantha. I'm so relieved that you've finally found someone." Her remark as she and Elizabeth were about to leave had Sam stammering like a schoolgirl.

"Oh, no, Mrs. Gautier, it's . . . that is . . ."

"Never mind, my dear," the older woman said soothingly. "There's no need to explain, no need at all. Your eyes tell the story so much better than words. And he seems genuinely fond of Elizabeth," she prattled on, leaving a stunned Sam to stare at her retreating back as she hurried across the flagstone patio and through the gate in the brick wall that surrounded the minuscule courtyard at the rear of Sam's house.

My eyes? Sam asked herself incredulously. My eyes? "Oh, Lord," she murmured under her breath as she scurried back inside and raced to the bathroom. Once there, she locked the door and then crossed the short distance to the mirror. She peered critically at her reflection, paying close attention to her eyes.

Other than a rosy glow in her cheeks, there didn't seem to be any difference. Her eyes were the same emerald green as they'd always been. Poor dear, Sam thought fondly of her elderly friend. She's such a romantic, she sees what she wants to. There was an exhaled breath of relief that no visible signs of her love for Greg were in evidence.

Sam was unaware that the becoming color in her cheeks, the sparkle in her eyes, spoke louder than words ever could. She'd have been shocked had she known that to others she did indeed have the "look" of a woman in love, as well as that special serenity that comes from having been made love to by an expert.

The morning passed quickly for Sam, caught up as she was in seeing the plans she'd so often envisioned coming to life before her very eyes. Her pleasure was further enhanced by Greg's presence and the fact that he was responsible for . . . in more ways than one . . . the dreamlike state she found herself in.

Each time their eyes met, the touch of his fingers as he unconsciously sought her slim hand in a warm clasp, or the casual shrug of an arm across her shoulders as he explained some phase of the work being done, drew Sam further and further under the spell of his compelling magic.

The other men, expecially Sean, were well aware of the blue sparks of electricity flying between their employer and his ex-wife. They were also aware of the need for discretion, and Greg's unspoken trust that they would respect that. Their loyalty was limitless. Privately they considered their boss to be slightly unhinged to have let Sam get away the first time.

The only moment of tension throughout the hectic morning occurred with Jim's arrival. Sam made a point as she introduced him to Greg of mentioning that Jim had only been with the firm for approximately two years, in case Greg jumped to any conclusions that he had been around at the time of their divorce.

In spite of all her fears, Greg accepted Jim's presence with friendly interest, after observing the casual relationship that existed between Sam and her easygoing coworker.

On one hurried trip to the kitchen to get a pair of pliers for Jim, Sam met Greg in the narrow hallway. The smile of gratitude she threw him didn't go unnoticed. Instead of stepping aside and allowing her to pass, he deliberately blocked her path, his tall frame absorbing the impact of her small body with no visible signs of expended effort.

"What's that lovely smile in favor of?" he asked huskily, his large hands sliding down her spine and stopping on the gentle swell of her hips.

Sam slipped her arms around his waist, her upper body leaning slightly backward as she gazed into his face. "Partly for being so nice to Jim," she told him, not even attempting to hide her pleasure.

"And the other?" he persisted.

She grinned, suddenly wary of the direction the conversation had taken. "I think you're fishing for a compliment," she teased, hoping to distract his attention from his question. Greg had a unique way of forcing the heightened awareness that existed between them.

"I am," he agreed bluntly, bringing his hands up to frame her face. He touched his mouth to hers, his tongue lazily outlining the fullness of her lips. Sam was shaken by his sensual attack on her senses, drugged by the masculine scent of his heated body.

Suddenly the licking and teasing wasn't enough. Lips that had been quivering in anticipation of a greater reward, parted under the surging demands of a more dominant force. Greg's tongue dipped into the honeyed sweetness of her mouth, drinking and plundering at will. There was a ruthless determination in his probing . . . a demand that she participate, a slight tremor coursing crazily throughout his massive body as she did so.

"Ahmmmmmm . . ." The amused voice came from directly behind Greg's broad shoulders. "Why don't you two find a room somewhere, preferably a bedroom," Sean drawled, one shoulder propped against the wall, his thumbs tucked into the waistband of his close-fitting jeans.

Greg recovered first, turning his head and staring frostily at the intruder. "Has anyone ever told you that your timing is lousy?" he snarled at his brother.

"Now that you mention it, no. But then, I'm not in the habit of interrupting steaming love scenes either." He grinned unrepentantly.

"Well," Greg said, "now that you've made your obnoxious presence known, what do you want?"

"We're almost ready to start moving the furniture upstairs and could use your help. I also didn't think you'd want to be a peep show for the rest of the men."

Greg glowered, but refrained from commenting. Sam, after the initial embarrassment of being caught in a heated embrace, was finding it difficult to control her amusement at his discomfort. To be caught necking in a hallway was a new experience for Greg, and one he found to be very disagreeable.

Later, as she was supervising the placement of the bedroom furniture, Sean managed to catch her alone in Elizabeth's room.

"I'm sorry if I embarrassed you back there, Sam,"

he said, taking the stack of blankets she was struggling with and storing them on one of the shelves in the closet. He turned back to her and grinned. "I've never seen Greg at such a loss for words."

She chuckled. "I agree. But I'd stay out of his way for a while if I were you. How about putting these suitcases on that shelf above the one the blankets are on?"

Sean easily dealt with the cases, then stepped back, his hands on his hips as he surveyed the room. The pale blue walls, the finish on the loose-woven paneling, was bright and cheery. Sam was using the same white dust ruffle on the bed and the frilly white curtains at the window.

"You've done a nice job in here. I really like it."

"Thank you. But you sound skeptical." She smiled at the offhanded compliment. "Were you expecting feathers and beads?"

Sean shrugged. "You know how some decorators are. They come in and take over. A friend of mine had his apartment redone recently." He shook his head. "Honest, Sam, it looks like a cross between the front parlor of a house of ill repute and a fortune teller's holy of holies. The poor guy almost went into cardiac arrest when he walked in and saw it for the first time."

Sam laughed, amazed at how easily she and Sean had resumed their former relationship. She also remembered, fondly, that it was Sean who had sought her out when he was in Dallas on business.

During the course of dinner . . . an invitation he'd refused to allow her to ignore . . . he'd severely criticized his brother, calling him seven kinds of a fool. Sam appreciated his support, of course, but her heart had been like a block of ice, numbed by her bitter experience. Their paths hadn't crossed again till that day in Antoine's.

Greg, hearing their laughter and their voices raised in one of the harmless arguments that always went on when they were together, stood in the doorway watching. There was an odd expression of wistfulness etched in the rugged features of his face as he deliberately became an eavesdropper.

As he reached up to clasp the back of his neck with one hand the flicker of movement caught Sam's attention. She threw him a relaxed smile. "Looking for something to do?" she asked saucily, catching a fleeting glimpse of the play of emotions across his face.

"What do you have in mind?" The ambiguity of the question was not lost on Sam as she watched him swiftly composing his features into a mask of pleasant friendliness.

She paused in arranging the various articles on the floor of the closet and sat back on her heels, her arms bracing her body, palms flat against the floor, as she subjected him to a deliberate scrutiny. "I suppose that depends on you, doesn't it? In my limited experience I've learned that it's best to tackle the most difficult chore first. Once that's sorted out, the smaller ones seem to fall into place with a minimum of effort."

"I see," Greg replied quietly, moving into the room and coming to a halt beside her. "Does this theory of yours always work?" he asked, his sensuous mouth curving cynically.

"Until lately I never doubted its validity." Instead of continuing to force her head back in an uncomfortable position in order to see him, Sam slid backwards until her back was resting against the foot of the bed. She relaxed against the solid support and drew her knees up to her chest.

Sean, once again an unwilling witness to the conflict between them, slowly shook his head. "Er . . . if you'll excuse me, I believe I'll see how the work is coming along," he announced, chuckling when neither Sam nor Greg paid the slightest heed to his departure.

Greg followed Sam's lead, opting for the edge of the bed rather than the floor, the firmness of one denim-clad thigh pressing against her shoulder as he leaned forward, his elbows resting on his knees. "What great decisions are you facing . . . other than finishing the work on this house?"

There was a slight pause before she let her head drop against the cushioned softness of the mattress. Her green eyes were partially hidden by the thickly fringed lashes as she studied him. "My main objective in returning to New Orleans."

"And that is?"

"To prove to you, once and for all, that I was not having an affair with Claude." There was a determined thrust to the angle of her jaw, the stubborn set of her chin, as two pairs of green eyes met and held.

"Why is absolving yourself of guilt so important?"

"Not absolving myself of guilt, Greg. There is no guilt waiting to be exorcised from some supposedly tortuous caverns of my mind. My deepest regret is that I didn't stay and fight."

"There was quite a bit of evidence against you, Samantha. Some that I don't think you're aware of even now," Greg told her, his voice gruff with emotion. "Why not let it die. We've both managed to survive. Doesn't that count for something?"

"I suppose it does . . . if you're willing to live the rest of your life under a cloud of suspicion. But I'm not. I learned a lot from John. . . . No, Greg, don't go all cold and icy at the mention of his name," she lashed out bluntly. "You would have liked him. He was a fine person. He did more for me in our brief time together than an analyst could have accomplished in a year."

"Samantha, John might have been a saint, a veritable paragon of virtue, but there's no way in hell that I would have liked him," Greg retorted hotly. "He held you in his arms, made love to you. In my book that's an automatic elimination from the ranks of people I consider my friends!"

"But you never even knew him!"

"A fact for which I'm heartily grateful," he snapped. "The only result of your union with your beloved John that pleases me . . . is Elizabeth."

"I see," Sam said crisply, rising to her feet in one smooth, graceful motion. She stood before him, her small fists planted on her hips. "Then what has all this been in aid of, Greg?" she demanded, waving one hand toward the suite of rooms. "We've been together almost continuously for the past week. Has the time you've spent with me been some sort of . . . self-imposed punishment?"

"Dammit, that's enough," he growled, getting to his feet in a swift bound, his large hands dropping to her shoulders in a decisive grip. "You know damn well why I'm here, so don't play the innocent with me. You're still a part of me and I want you." The admission was dragged painfully from him.

"But?" she boldly challenged, daring him to voice his true feelings.

"Leave it, Samantha." The rough sound of his voice brought a curious glitter of frustration to her eyes.

She stared up at his face, the hell he was suffering reflected in the taut muscles, the rigid set of his jaw. "Nothing I've said or done has made the slightest difference in your thinking, has it, Greg?"

Deep down there was a heart-wrenching twinge of despair. For no matter how close they became, there would always be that doubt, that look in his eyes when their gazes met that betrayed his lack of faith in her. In that instant Sam was forced to admit that no love, regardless of how strong, could withstand the creeping erosion of doubt and the steady deterioration of their lives.

She inhaled deeply, a sad twist pulling at the gentle curve of her mouth. "I'm sorry, Greg, so very sorry. I suppose that in my naive way of looking at things, I assumed that when we did see each other, you'd realize just how wrong you'd been to ever doubt me."

"Whether or not I trust you doesn't alter the fact that I still love you, Samantha," Greg said dully. He stepped around her and walked over to stare out the window, the grim line of his profile offering no compromise. "I'd deliberately put off seeing you, knowing that when I did, I wouldn't be able to stop." He swung round and faced her. "Even now I want you to marry me. The thought of you and Elizabeth on your own scares the living hell out of me. I want to protect you, care for you."

Sam briefly closed her eyes against the proposal. She couldn't help but be pleased, but her victory was short-lived. What he was offering, or so it seemed to her, was that they simply disregard the eroding undercurrent of lies and distrust between them. With him nursing his bruised ego, dropping the occasional wounding remark, and her struggling every day to prove her faithfulness and slowly dying from the look of pain in his eyes.

As much as she wanted Greg, she knew she couldn't endure such agony. They would end up two embittered people, their lives destroyed.

"I'm sorry, Greg. But it's all or nothing. I've no intention of passing a life sentence on myself for a crime I never committed." Sam turned and walked from the room on leaden feet.

CHAPTER NINE

At the end of the day, Sam was mentally and physically exhausted, and from the moment she'd walked away from Greg, she'd felt the heavy blanket of depression enveloping her like a black cloud.

If the others were aware of the strained atmosphere between Sam and Greg, they were careful to hide it, continuing to treat Sam in the same easygoing manner that they had for most of the day.

By the time the others were gone and she was left alone with Greg, her endurance had been stretched to the breaking point. There was a frosty politeness in the air as they tackled the job of cleaning up. To her protest that she could handle it, Greg had simply replied, "Shut up!" After that terse request they worked side by side like two well-trained robots.

Eventually and mercifully it was time for him to leave. Sam stood in the center of the living room, her hands tightly clenched against the trembling that no amount of silent lecturing could control.

She felt rather than saw Greg as he stopped mere inches behind her, the incredible male scent of him causing her stomach to lurch crazily.

The sudden touch of his fingers against the softness of her nape brought a startled shiver from Sam, a scattering of goose pimples along the slimness of her arms. "Don't look so forlorn, dammit," he muttered in a savage undertone. "It's not going to stop here, I can't let it."

The fingers that had been gently stroking now slid through the riot of dark curls. His other hand caught her by the upper arm and slowly turned her to face him.

"One way or the other, I intend to have you and Elizabeth with me. I want you in my bed . . . and I intend to adopt your daughter."

"And if I happen not to want the same thing?" Sam forced herself to meet his probing gaze.

"Oh . . . but you do, baby. There's nothing on earth that can change that." His lips touched hers in a kiss that was tender and brief. They were both emotionally drained, their passion smoldering beneath the rubble of confusion that surrounded them.

"I won't press you tonight, but I'll expect you to have dinner with me tomorrow evening. I'll pick you up at eight o'clock sharp."

142

"I usually don't go out during the week, Greg. I hate leaving Elizabeth." She grasped the first thought that entered her head. She could have saved her breath for all the good it did her.

"That's a pitiful excuse, and you know it. Elizabeth is in bed and asleep long before eight, Samantha." He eyed her intently. "Anything else?" he asked, perfectly aware that she was grasping at straws.

"I suppose not," Sam tartly replied, resentment flaring up at his open manipulation of her. She glared at him in angry silence. "Are you sure you want to be seen with me? I mean . . . there are times when it's rather difficult to cover the huge A emblazoned on my forehead."

"I'll risk it, Samantha," he answered, his amused, indulgent chuckle ringing over her head. "I'm sure you'll rise to the occasion."

Sam wanted desperately, achingly, to tell him to go to hell, but knew it would be a futile waste of breath. Not to mention that she would, in all probability, follow him if he did.

"Would you like for me to go next door and bring Elizabeth home?" he asked, ignoring her sulkiness.

"No!" she snapped and then was immediately contrite. Regardless of his personal opinion of her, he had put in a long, hard weekend, and all for her benefit. "I'm sorry, Greg. I didn't mean to sound so crabby."

"Think nothing of it, honey. Although"—he

stared at her through shuttered lids, his hands expertly kneading the tired muscles of her shoulders—"it might be a good idea if I stayed over tonight. You need me to make love to you in the worst possible way. You're like a high-strung filly, your body is quivering in my hands, begging me to calm you down."

"Why you conceited ba—"she stammered, only to have Greg's unrestrained laughter stop her.

"Don't be embarrassed for wanting me, sweetheart. I assure you the feeling is mutual."

Sam's cheeks were still burning with outraged indignation several minutes later as she scooted out the back door and through the wrought-iron gate to bring Elizabeth home.

Damn him! she thought disconsolately, heaping a silent litany of abuse on his insufferable head as she crossed the yard. I'm vulnerable and he knows it. She also knew he wouldn't be adverse to using that vulnerability to get his own way. The determined fervor with which she'd started out in her attempt to win back Greg's love was suddenly losing its appeal. Marriage to him with only a physical relationship binding them together would never work. Or would it?

The next morning as she sat at her desk Sam was finding it difficult to concentrate, staring unseeingly at the open file before her. Greg's face was superimposed on each sheet of paper she picked up. Finally, after staring dumbly at a job estimation that had made perfect sense when she first drew it up but had suddenly become almost indecipherable, she slumped back wearily in her chair and stared into space.

Her thoughts resembled a wildly spinning wheel, a mad kaleidoscope of Greg's rugged features in various expressions . . . ranging from anger, rage . . . to incredible gentleness as he made love to her. He was slowly driving her crazy, and she was helpless to stop him.

Even in thought, the memory of his hands stroking her body, the touch of his lips, pulled at the tight coil of desire in her stomach. She wanted him with a stark, primitive craving that shocked her to her very core. She also had a sneaking feeling that whether or not Greg ever believed in her, he would play a dominant role in her future.

It was in this muddled state that Claude found her. He paused in the doorway and stared intently at the dreamy expression on the heart-shaped face. "Have you snagged a choice commission or are you simply indulging in pleasant daydreams?" he asked as he closed the door and walked over and took a seat on the corner of her desk.

Sam threw him a startled look, then quickly assumed an unconvincing air of brisk professional interest. "Hello, Claude. What can I do for you?" she asked, neatly sidestepping the innocently posed question. "Are you feeling better?"

"Oh, yes, I'm much better. It was only a slight

flareup," he reassured her. "Jim tells me he installed the carpet in your addition yesterday. I wasn't aware that you'd progressed so far." There was a faintly accusing tone in his voice that puzzled Sam.

Claude had been most helpful with his suggestions, had even let her buy the carpet, wallpaper, and paneling through the firm at cost. Perhaps he was feeling left out.

"Things have gone a bit faster than I'd anticipated," she smiled. "It's beginning to look as though I'll be through well before Thanksgiving."

"Jim also mentioned that he met someone named Howland . . . yesterday at your place. Of course I immediately discounted that bit of erroneous information." He smiled thinly, letting the slight flaring of his nostrils express his disapproval. "Exactly who were the men you hired? I don't recall you asking me for the names of the carpenters I'd lined up for you."

Suddenly there was an air of tension in the room that was uncomfortable. Sam stared at Claude, aware of and at the same time unable to explain the shaft of apprehension that transfixed her. "Jim wasn't mistaken, Claude. Greg has been helping me. In fact, he and Sean worked all day Saturday and Sunday. They brought over two other men as well. I'm sure you'll be pleased with the results."

"Hardly pleased, Samantha," he grated, his thin lips clamping into a rigid scowl of disapproval. "I never dreamed you'd be so foolish as to allow Greg Howland back into your life."

146

"I'm not sure he ever left, Claude."

"How totally maudlin!" he exclaimed harshly, the cool facade that had become his trademark beginning to crumble. "He treated you abominably, Samantha—not even waiting until you left the city before falling into Monica's arms."

"Claude!" Sam spoke sharply. "I really don't care to discuss Greg with you. All I'm concerned with at the moment is proving to him that I wasn't unfaithful to him. I don't want to hear any old stories . . . old accusations."

Claude rose to his feet, the icy glitter in his gray eyes like a burst of Arctic air as he stared at Sam. "You're making a horrible mistake by becoming involved with Greg again. I'm sure you're nothing more than a pleasant little diversion between mistresses. Besides, don't you think it's rather common? After all, he was all too obvious in his contempt for you. It should be patently clear, my dear, that his interest now can only lead to one thing . . . a seamy little affair."

For a brief moment after his angry tirade Sam sat in stunned silence. The insulting remarks, the deliberate innuendos, had been part of Claude's personality that had remained carefully hidden over the years. Gone was the precise gentleman, the courteous employer and friend. The person staring at her across the width of her desk was a total stranger . . . vicious and brutal in his attack.

"Are you quite finished?" she asked softly, clenching her fists beneath the desk as she struggled for control. Only their years of close friendship kept Sam from telling him exactly where he could go . . . and what he could do with his opinions! The hurt he'd inflicted by forcing into the open things she'd tried desperately to forget would have to be dealt with later.

"Of course," he remarked stiffly, his face taking on an alarming pallor. "Why should my feelings be considered? After all, I'm merely the devoted friend . . . always around, ready to pick up the pieces after the great Greg Howland has used you and then tossed you aside like some common tramp!"

"That's enough, Claude!" Sam cried, standing up so quickly that her chair slammed against the wall. "Friend or no, I refuse to be insulted by you. I can certainly appreciate your concern, but you've forgotten one important thing . . . *it is my life.*"

All the while she was speaking, Claude's breathing had become quite heavy, the faint rasping as he drew breath into his lungs growing louder and louder. Instead of replying to her firm request to mind his own business, he turned and walked unsteadily toward the door, one hand clutching the front of his shirt.

"Claude?" All anger left Sam's voice as she became aware of his alarming condition. She darted around the corner of the desk and hurried to his side. "Are you all right?" she asked, one hand going solicitously to his arm.

"Of course," he stiffly replied, pulling away as though her touch were contaminating. "I'm perfectly fine," he sniffed, and walked out.

Sam stared fixedly at the door, not sure if she should go after him or warn Libbie to keep an eye on him. She knew that emotionally she wasn't up to seeing him so soon after his furious attack on her. And yet she couldn't stand by and say nothing, especially in light of his medical history.

She turned and retraced her steps to her desk, reached for the receiver, and buzzed the receptionist. "Libbie, can you come to my office?"

Ten minutes later Libbie stared incredulously at Sam, then sank onto the only other available chair in the office. "Heavens, Samantha! I never dreamed . . . I mean . . ." She shook her head. "He's always so calm. The only time I've ever seen Claude upset is when some of his precious material has been roughly handled or a shipment of something is late." She chewed on her bottom lip, watching Sam as she paced. "You do grasp the meaning behind his outburst, don't you?"

"I'm trying not to," she ruefully retorted. "I keep hoping that it's honest concern. But he was so vicious. It's as though he denounced me . . . cast me out of his life, his thoughts . . . his mind."

"What are you going to do?"

"I'm not sure. For a woman who . . . only a week ago was leading a relatively uneventful life, I've suddenly acquired more problems than a dog has fleas."

Libbie smiled. Far from being surprised by Greg's presence at Samantha's home, the receptionist was dying to know what progress the two had made. However, Sam looked as though she'd had about all the harassment she could handle for one day.

"What's on your schedule for the day?" Libbie asked, reaching for the leather-bound desk calendar and pulling it forward. After assuring herself that most of the appointments could be rescheduled for later in the week, she turned back to Sam.

"Take the next couple of days off, honey. There's nothing here," she said, indicating the calendar, "that I can't easily shuffle. As for Claude," she quietly remarked, "who knows?"

"Two days sounds awfully tempting . . . and I think I'll do it."

"Elizabeth?"

"Mrs. Gautier is taking her to the zoo."

"Then be thankful for small favors. You need to be alone for a while," Libbie wisely advised.

Sam unlocked the back door and let herself into the kitchen, the quiet of her small house sweeping over her like a soothing balm. She dropped purse and keys on the table, then walked over to the stove and turned on the flame beneath the kettle.

On her way through the house she picked up several toys and carried them upstairs, dropping them into the toy box in Elizabeth's room. In her own bedroom Sam quickly changed from the attractive yellow blazer, white silk blouse, and cream-colored skirt to a pair of red slacks and a long-sleeved, red-and-white knit top.

Her only further concession to the chill in the air was a pair of tennis socks. After putting the clothes she'd just taken off on hangers and hanging them in the closet, she went back downstairs and into the kitchen.

There was much to be said for the calming effects of a hot cup of tea, Sam mused some time later as she relaxed on the sofa, her feet propped up on the edge of the coffee table. And at this particular point in her life she needed all the restorative elixirs she could get her hands on.

She'd been so confident . . . so sure of Claude's friendship. She'd never dreamed how deeply he resented Greg. She shook her head, still dazed by his outburst. There were numerous questions pulling at her thoughts, but the obvious answers were too ludicrous to consider.

He'd been unable to hide his contempt, leaving her feeling like something unclean. She wasn't even sure now that she wanted to continue working for Claude. That aspect of the situation wasn't daunting. She'd had offers before from other firms eager for her services, knowing her name and her list of credits would enhance their reputations as well as add numerous accounts to their books.

No, it wasn't the lack of faith in her ability that

made the thought of changing jobs so distasteful, but the reasoning behind the chilling thought. . . .

Claude had been her mentor. Under his expert tutelage Sam had reached a plateau in her career that was envied by her peers. In a sense he had become almost godlike, her respect and admiration for his knowledge, as well as his personal friendship, unquestionable. To have him suddenly turn on her was mind-boggling; it had left her stunned and confused.

The day dragged on with unmerciful slowness. Sam puttered about the house in a halfhearted attempt at cleaning and dusting. But even the changes that had been made by knocking out the walls and transforming the downstairs into a large, sunny area failed to arouse her creative instincts. She worked without seeing a mental picture of the completion of the project, her hands performing tasks out of habit, her mind dulled and fuzzy.

By the time Greg arrived, Sam had managed to pull herself together . . . outwardly, her features a pleasant, smiling mask as she invited him in.

His gaze reflected undisguised male approval as it swept over the green dress she was wearing. Her only jewelry was an exquisite diamond pendant on a gold chain, the brillance of the stone intensified by the delicate filigree setting that surrounded it. The necklace had been a birthday present from Greg shortly after they were married.

There was a curious gleam of satisfaction in his eyes as he stared at the pendant. "So you did keep it." His slightly roughened palms cupped her face as he bent and kissed her with a passionate intensity that immediately had her clinging to the hardness of his arms for support.

"Enough of that." Greg eased her backward, his hands gripping her smooth upper arms, steadying her slightly limp body. "If you want to eat, Samantha, I suggest we get going. Otherwise"—his voice was grim with self-control—"I'm going to undress you and make love to you. What's it to be?"

Sam's face turned a delicate shade of pink at this blunt speech, but then . . . that was Greg. He wasn't the type of man to hide his desire for a woman. "You're still as outspoken as ever, aren't you?" Her mouth quirked into a smile as she walked over and picked up the ecru lace shawl and the small beaded bag.

"With you I'd feel rather foolish being anything else," he retorted, a scowl darkening his face. "Where you're concerned, I've yet to master the art of self-control."

"Poor Greg," Sam murmured teasingly, letting her fingertips trail softly across the firm thrust of his stubborn chin as she swept past him and out the door.

"You do enjoy living dangerously, don't you, Samantha?" he growled as he cupped her elbow and led her to his car. "Perhaps you'd be better off plotting your escape rather than spending your time teasing me."

"Me? A tease?" she exclaimed innocently, a tiny beguiling smile pulling at the softness of her mouth. "Why, Greg, how ungentlemanly of you."

"Gentleman be damned!" he snarled, closing her door, then walking around and getting in behind the wheel. "If it was a gentleman you wanted, why didn't you grab Claude Favret?"

"If you were a woman, I'd tell you to sheathe your claws," Sam calmly informed him. "As it stands, I'll simply remind you that I've had ample time to catch Claude. If you weren't such a stubborn, thickheaded fool, you'd see that without my having to point it out."

"I see."

"I doubt it, Greg. I seriously doubt it," Sam said scathingly.

Ten minutes later Greg switched off the engine of the car in the underground garage of his apartment building. The restaurant they were going to was in the heart of the French Quarter. Since his apartment was close by, parking in the garage was much better than searching for space on a street some distance from their destination.

Greg turned to Sam, his arm snaking along the top of the seat, his hand clasping her nape and forcing her to look at him. Instead of the brooding anger she was expecting, Sam was surprised to see mischief brimming in his green eyes, a devilish grin on his face.

"If this stubborn, thickheaded . . . er . . ."

154

"Fool," Sam readily supplied.

Greg grimaced. "All right . . . fool . . . promises not to ruin the evening with snide insinuations about your employer, will you exchange that frown for a smile?"

Sam tilted her head consideringly, one forefinger resting against her chin as she struggled to maintain a thoughtful pose. "What are you offering?"

"Offering?"

"As an inducement, Greg. Surely you can't expect a blanket capitulation without offering me a suitable inducement." She met his smoldering gaze with her own softly veiled one, which contained a hint of mystery, a promise of sensual pleasure to come.

There was restrained savagery in Greg as he slowly and deliberately pulled Sam into his arms. For a brief moment, before his lips closed on hers, the spicy aroma of expensive after-shave, mixed with the familiar male scent of him, caused her body to quiver in anticipation.

His mouth moved hungrily over hers, pillaging and ravishing the warm, dark sweetness. His tongue became the master in the artful game of thrust and parry. Teasing, taunting . . . seeking and receiving a response that rocked them both.

When Greg drew back, the sound of his tortured breathing was loud in the closeness of the car. They stared at each other in awed wonder, the depth of feeling charged the very air they breathed, precluded the need for words.

With a gentleness that brought a shimmer of tears to her eyes, Sam felt Greg's hands smoothing the bodice of her dress in place . . . the fleeting touch as his fingers brushed back an errant curl that had fallen across her forehead.

"Marry me, Samantha," he whispered. "Take me out of this hell I've been existing in for three damnable years."

"Oh, Greg," she murmured softly, reaching out and caressing the curve of his lips with her thumb. "You say that now, but what comes later?"

"Do you love me, Samantha?"

"You know I do."

"Then promise me you'll think about it. What our love can be . . . the happiness that can be ours. Will you do that?" He bent forward and traced the outline of her lips with the moist tip of his tongue.

"Mmm . . ." Sam achingly groaned. "Is this your inducement?" she whispered.

"Is it working?" he asked huskily, his hands adding their own encouragement as they slid lazily over the thrust of her small, firm breasts, the arched curve of her spine.

"You could say that. I'll let you know in an hour or two." She closed her eyes and luxuriated in the pleasure he was giving her. "Ouch!" Her reverie was rudely shattered by a sharp whack on her silk-clad behind.

"You, Greg Howland, are a monster!" Sam exclaimed, eyeing him warily across the few inches that now separated them.

"I'm not and you know it, you shameless wanton. But I refuse to go to my apartment and take a cold shower in order to have dinner. In fact, I've had more damned cold showers in the last ten days than in my entire life!"

"Serves you right, you heavy-handed lout." She grinned in spite of herself at the scowling expression that clouded his face. It was a heady sensation, this newfound power she had to excite him. It had always been there, but Sam had been safe in his love, or so she thought, preferring that he be the aggressor . . . the one to set the tone of their lovemaking.

Now she was a woman, one who had plummeted from the peaks of heaven to the depths of despair. She was no longer a willing follower but a woman with strong needs and desires of her own. Desires that only one man could fulfill, that man being Greg.

CHAPTER TEN

"Oh," Sam sighed, "I do adore this place." She leaned back in her chair, replete with delicious food, excellent wine. And now, coffee with a generous dollop of whipped cream crowning the dark brew. "I feel absolutely decadent." She smiled at Greg across the intimate table for two. The mellowed beauty of the historic old restaurant added the perfect backdrop to their first real dinner together.

"No comment." Greg grinned.

"I repeat, you are not a gentleman." She pouted at his teasing put-down.

Greg shook his head, a woeful expression on his face. "Keep talking, Samantha. My list of grievances against you is growing to astronomical proportions."

"I've never been out with a man who kept a list of

my indiscretions. What do you intend to do with it?" she asked innocently, flirting outrageously and enjoying every minute of it.

"Rest assured, you'll know soon enough, little one. Then we'll see how brave you really are. By the way, have I told you how lovely you are tonight?" His eyes caressed her with their warmth, making love to her without even touching her.

Sam could feel the tips of her breasts harden, hear the blood rushing through her veins as she succumbed to the heady intensity of his emerald gaze. "No, you haven't," she murmured in a voice barely audible above the muted din of the other patrons. "Thank you."

"Where were you today? I called you three different times. Your friend Libbie was either being close-mouthed as hell about your whereabouts or getting some perverse pleasure out of not telling me."

Sam debated whether or not to tell him about Claude, finally deciding against it. The situation was explosive enough without any additional prodding on her part. "I . . . I was at home," she finally managed. "Things were slow, and I decided to take the day off. I'll probably do the same tomorrow."

"Then why the mystery?" he asked, uncannily alert to the abrupt change in her mood, her hesitancy in meeting his gaze. "I seem to recall hearing you and Jim discussing several things that needed taking care of today. Did you cancel all your appointments?"

"No, I didn't. Libbie rescheduled them for later in

the week." She risked a cautious look at him. "Let's drop it, shall we? There are much more interesting subjects to discuss than my work."

"What happened, Samantha?" The question almost shattered her calm with its deliberateness.

"Nothing *happened*, Greg. Good heavens"—she laughed nervously—"can't a girl take a couple of days off without its becoming a national scandal?"

"In your case . . . no," he remarked icily, never taking his eyes off her face. Then he totally unnerved her by asking, very solicitously, if she cared for anything else.

"No . . . no, thank you." Sam smiled, relieved. "I couldn't possibly eat another bite."

"Good." Greg returned her smile, then signaled the waiter in an unobtrusive manner for the bill.

To Sam, the entire scenario . . . from the moment he asked where she had been all day to the moment she found herself being seated in the car couldn't have taken more than five minutes.

She watched Greg's determined stride as he walked around the front of the car, jerked open the door, and slid into the driver's seat. His implacable profile revealed little of what he was thinking . . . other than a slow-burning rage that seemed to be enveloping his entire being. It was obvious from the rigid set of his massive shoulders beneath the superb-fitting dark suit, from the way his large capable hands gripped the steering wheel.

"Greg, I—"

"Later, Samantha. We'll discuss it later." He cut her off, his speech short and clipped.

Sam had no choice but to comply with his wishes. She sat quietly as he drove through the French Quarter.

There were crowds at the entrances of the various clubs, some gawking at the provocative glimpses they were allowed of the nude dancers, others waiting to be admitted. The music ranged from really good jazz to the rhythmic monotony that accompanied the dancers. The mood was entirely different from the daylight scene of charming wrought-iron balconies, Jackson Square, antique stores, and hidden courtyards protecting centuries-old secrets.

Throughout the entire drive Greg remained as silent as a post. Instead of parking on the street in front of Sam's house, he turned into the alley behind it, stopping the dark blue Mercedes next to her Volvo.

"Why don't you put on a pot of coffee while I get Elizabeth?" he suggested, and Sam sighed with relief. It would give her a chance to figure out some plausible explanation for having played truant from a job he knew to be extremely demanding.

After getting the coffee going, Sam hurried upstairs to her bedroom and changed out of the green dress into a caftan in a delicate shade of pink, a perfect foil for her fair complexion and dark hair.

She met Greg as she was coming out of her bedroom. He waved aside her offer to tuck Elizabeth in.

Again she offered no protest, glad for the extended reprieve.

It was only after they were seated on the sofa, a tray with coffeepot and gaily painted mugs on the low table in front of them, that Greg . . . minus his jacket and tie, his shirt opened several buttons, turned his dark head toward Sam. "Well?"

She replied in kind from her lounging position beside him, both with their feet propped up on the coffee table. "Well what?" She resented his nosy attitude.

"What happened to send you home? And Samantha . . . don't bother denying that something did. Your face is an open book."

"I'd really rather not go into it, Greg. It's personal, and the less said, the better."

"All right, if that's the way you want it. But, remember, I did ask you first," Greg replied matter-of-factly. He drew his arms up, crossing his hands behind his head, watching Sam from between half-closed lids. "I'll go see Claude first thing in the morning. What time does he usually get to the shop?"

"Greg, please!" she cried, scrambling around like a small, excited kitten as she jackknifed into a sitting position and drew her feet up under her. "I don't want you involved in this." Visions of him throttling Claude in a fit of rage flashed before her eyes. She also knew Greg was just itching to settle a hypothetical score with the older man as well.

"But I am involved, honey. With any and everything that concerns you and Elizabeth. You unwittingly issued a challenge that day in Antoine's, and I gladly accepted."

Sam recognized only too well the unshakable, steely quality of his voice, disguised by the velvet tones. He was thoroughly intimidating, and she knew that one way or another, he'd get an answer to his question.

"Will you promise to stay out of it if I tell you what happened?" she asked, not at all convinced that telling him was the right thing to do. "Will you let me handle it in my own way?

"That depends, honey," he said quietly yet uncompromisingly. "Why not tell me? We'll sort out the rest later. Okay?"

"No, it's not okay," Sam muttered belligerently, moving away from him to the very end of the sofa. "But then . . . that's the way it's always been with you, isn't it, Greg? You vacillate between bulldozing your way over people and cleverly manipulating them. Well, remember one thing, I won't stand for either."

"Whatever you say, Samantha. Now . . . tell me what happened," he said with maddening calm.

"I had a terrible fight with Claude," she replied in a small, quiet voice, her eyes riveted on her nervous fingers, which were pleating and alternately smoothing the fabric of her gown. "Jim let it slip that you were over here Sunday. When Claude asked me about it, I told him that not only were you here

Sunday, but that you and Sean had been working over here the entire weekend. He was livid." She exhaled sharply, giving a resigned shrug of her shoulders. "Before it was over, he said some things I'm not sure I can forget. I'm seriously considering quitting as well."

"What did he say?" Greg asked, so softly that Sam barely heard him.

"That you were only using me . . . that I was insane to let you back into my life . . . that you'd toss me aside like a common tramp."

"Don't," Greg harshly demanded, reaching over and placing his slightly roughened palm against her lips. There was such an outpouring of anger emanating from his eyes that Sam shuddered. "I get the message." Before she could guess his intentions, she found herself being plucked from her distant position and tucked beneath his arm, her body pressed against the warmth of his side.

"Now," he rumbled, his arms locked about her, her face resting against his chest, "I think it's time we discussed a few facts regarding your good friend Claude. And you're right about quitting. I don't want you anywhere near that maniac. He is . . . and has been in love with you for years."

"But that's ridiculous!" Sam cried, bracing her hands against Greg's chest and staring up at him. "I don't care what lies Monica told you, Claude has never been anything but a devoted friend . . . until today."

164

"And you dare accuse me of wearing blinders?" he asked incredulously. "Samantha! Samantha! Your aging Lothario had just as much to do with our divorce as Monica."

"That's a terrible thing to say," she cried, trying to break free from the twin fetters of steel holding her. "He was as shocked as I was by your outrageous behavior. Let me go, Greg." She strained, to no avail, against his greater strength.

"I will not, and you may as well stop squirming. For once, you're going to listen to some plain, unvarnished facts about that slimy bastard you've idolized all these years."

"Hmph!" Sam snorted, settling back against his chest. "I doubt I'm likely to get any facts . . . varnished or otherwise, out of you where Claude is concerned," she muttered. "Only last week he told me how you almost attacked him when he went to your office and tried to explain why I'd stayed overnight at his apartment."

"Oh, he did, did he?" Greg hooted. "I'll say one thing for that two-faced son-of-a-bitch, he's got guts. Only this time I think he's overplayed his hand."

"What is that supposed to mean?"

"Claude didn't come to my office, I went to his. Apparently about the same time you went flying off to Reno. The news he was so eager to impart was that the two of you were lovers, and that as soon as the divorce was final, you'd be married. He repeated the same story he'd told Monica, correctly assuming she'd lose no time in informing me."

For the second time in one day Sam reeled from the impact of a severe shock, and her acceptance of the blow left her numb.

She knew she'd heard Greg correctly. His speech wasn't slurred, nor the words muffled. They had been starkly, painfully clear. In her heart she wanted to cry out in Claude's defense . . . wanted to lash out in anger . . . throw things, scream, demand that Greg take back his words.

But sadly, and with a feeling of dread that had been gnawing at her all day, Sam knew he wasn't lying. She remembered the almost maniacal gleam in Claude's face as the ugly accusations had rushed from his mouth. There was also the nagging discrepancy in the story he'd told about going to see Greg and attempting to explain. Even as she'd listened to him, Sam had found it difficult to imagine Claude braving an encounter with Greg, especially on the latter's home turf. Claude was certainly deficient in the stuff of which heroes are made.

"Samantha?" Greg's concerned voice rumbled deep in his chest. "Are you all right?"

All right? All right? No! she wanted to scream, I'm not all right. Because of the inexplicable deceit of two people she'd had three years of her life turned into a living hell. No . . . no, she quickly amended as hysteria began edging further and further into her being . . . not John and Elizabeth. Not John and

166

Elizabeth. Unaware, until she felt Greg shaking her, that she was whimpering that one phrase aloud in a desperate attempt to find some balance, some justification for the unfairness of it all.

"Samantha! Stop it!" One large hand lost itself in the curly thickness of her hair, the other gripped her shoulder. He forced her head back, swearing forcefully when he saw the tears that were overflowing the green pools of her eyes and easing down her face. "Samantha Ewing, if you're crying over that bastard Favret, I swear I'll beat the flaming hell out of you." The gruff timbre of his voice belied the threat. There was compassion in his eyes, his touch. Sam couldn't remember ever seeing Greg in such acute distress, and it was oddly amusing.

"No," she whispered. "I'm not crying for Claude, Greg. Quite the contrary. I will admit, however, that this has been a most memorable day."

Greg bent down and touched his lips to the salty wetness on her cheeks, then enfolded her to him as though she were the most important thing in the world.

Sam accepted the gentleness of his embrace like a drowning kitten seeking shelter in a storm. For the first time since the day she'd left him, she knew the untold relief of being in his arms without feeling she was on trial.

Yet . . . she wanted to hear it out loud. "Do you believe me?"

167

"Oh, yes, I believe you now. But I've been puzzled about several things for some time."

An alert stillness caught at Sam as she heard this almost casual admission. She drew far enough back to see his face, her eyes widened in outright bewilderment. "Exactly what are you puzzled about?" Her brows knit pensively as she waited.

"I suppose it started when you married John Ewing. That was a profound shock, Samantha, and one I'm not sure I've recovered from yet." His hands gripped her shoulders convulsively. "There I was, waiting for an announcement of your marriage to Claude Favret, and you damn near knocked me dead by marrying a total stranger."

He released her and then sat forward and reached for the coffeepot. After pouring a cup for each of them, he added sugar to his . . . cream and sugar to Sam's and handed her the hot brew. He remained where he was, his huge hands engulfing the mug. "Sean had been raising hell with me from the first, accusing me of being a fool . . . that I'd been taken in. I really think I was on the verge of breaking his neck when we heard from Jacques about you and John."

Greg took a sip of his coffee, set the mug back on the tray, then ran one hand through his hair. "I flew to Houston and took Monica out to dinner, determined to get some answers. I'm afraid I wasn't very nice. By the time I left her later in the evening, I'd gotten enough information out of her to know that indeed I'd been royally screwed." At that point he turned and looked over his shoulder at Sam. "I guess you could categorize my behavior for the next month or so as suicidal.

"I don't think I drew a sober breath for six weeks. It ended . . . mercifully so, with Sean stopping me from going to Claude's apartment and killing him after Monica told me everything. After that I began pulling myself back together. When I heard that Ewing was dead"—he slowly shook his head, his lips pulled tight against his teeth—"I was relieved. But the doubts came back when you returned to New Orleans and took up with Claude again."

"Oh, Greg darling . . ." Sam murmured, slipping to the edge of the sofa and hugging him, her face pressed against his shoulder. "Claude was never my reason for coming back. I just went back to work for him, nothing more."

Sam raised trembling fingers and lovingly stroked the harshness from the face she loved so much, smoothing and caressing every feature that had lived so vividly in her memory. "Why did you let me go on believing you still distrusted me?" She tapped him sharply on the chin and glowered. "That wasn't very nice, Mr. Howland."

"You didn't like that . . . mmmm?" He caught her hand and pressed the palm to his cheek. "Seriously though, I don't think you would have believed me if I told you Claude loved you, and like I said, I still had my doubts about how you felt about him. So I figured the best way to handle the situation was to play out my hand—that is, to find out the truth by sweeping you off your feet. That way I was fairly certain you and your 'friend' would react, and you both did."

"Ha!" Sam exclaimed. "I beg to differ with you, my love. For once in your nefarious life, you were the one getting swept, and I was wielding the broom. I hate to keep feeding that enormous ego of yours, but I came after you with a determination that even I wasn't aware of. But you, you fink." She frowned at him. "Do you have any idea how I've suffered?"

"All right, so I wasn't completely honest with you. But I was vulnerable as hell, woman. Here I'd been living the life of a monk—"

"A monk?" she cried disparagingly, raising herself up and supporting her weight on one elbow.

"So . . . I exaggerated a little. There were"—his eyes dancing mischievously—"women . . . occasionally . . ." He threw up an arm to ward off the well-aimed missile of Sam's small fist. "I hopped into bed with half the women in New Orleans, as well as other points in the continental United States and abroad!" he spat out in a mad rush. "Now . . . does that satisfy you, you nosy baggage?"

"Unfortunately . . . no," Sam sighed, resting her chin on his chest as she watched him. "However, celibacy is totally foreign to your character. But enough about your insatiable libido. Where is Monica?"

"I haven't the faintest idea. After I found out how she'd been plotting with Claude, I fired her."

"Why didn't you get in touch with me after John's death?" Sam demanded, determined to get an answer to all the questions that had plagued her.

"Claire assured me that you would be returning to New Orleans after Elizabeth was born." He smiled. "If you hadn't, I would have come to get you in Dallas. I felt I had to give you time to get over John's death. I didn't want any ghosts peeking over my shoulder. And then I found out Claude was back in your life."

"All the aforementioned is true. But I still detect a tiny urge for revenge hidden behind that facade of thoughtfulness. Am I correct?" Sam asked.

"How perceptive," Greg replied smoothly, too smoothly to suit Sam.

"You," she declared in ringing accents, "are a sneaky, underhanded, vengeful—"

Her tirade was abruptly halted when Greg grabbed her and pulled her over on top of him. His fingers cradled the back of her head and drew it forward, forcing her parted lips to meet his hungry mouth.

The thought of berating him was forgotten as she responded to the force of his love that was swiftly igniting a raging flame of desire from the tips of her toes to the top of her head.

Suddenly she was dumped on the cushioned softness of the sofa with Greg towering over her. Before she had time to question his intentions, Sam felt herself being swept up in his arms. As he strode toward the wrought-iron staircase she could hear the wild beating of his heart beneath her ear.

His stride didn't break until he reached the dimly lit bedroom and the satin-covered bed. There he eased her to the floor with deliberate slowness, her body sliding with an intensified sense of contact against his aroused flesh. His eyes revealed such need and longing for her that Sam felt an uncontrollable quivering all through her body.

Greg's movements were hurried but deft as he worked open the tiny row of buttons at the neckline of the caftan, then pushed it off her shoulders and down over her hips.

Sensing her intense need for him, he momentarily forsook the crested peaks and the valley between for the dark, mysterious treasure below. His thumbs hooked inside the fragile band of the wispy bikini panties, directly beneath the pivotal points of her hips.

With a silken whisper of movement the last remaining garment gave way to his invasion of her body . . . her senses.

Sam moved in a thrusting, arching rhythm against the hand that was now probing between her gleaming white thighs, searching for the strong, blunt-tipped fingers that were alternately stroking and touching the very essence of her sensuality.

Unable to withstand the fever of excitement that

172

was consuming her, Sam's hands began to frantically pull at Greg's shirt, not content until she felt the crisp hair that covered his chest, rough against her throbbing breasts . . . beneath the tips of her questing fingers.

She sought and found the two small points of arousal nestled in the midst of the dark growth, laving the rigid peak of first one and then the other with the tip of her hot pink tongue.

Their breathing was labored with excitement as the tide of passion irrevocably advanced, lapping closer and closer.

In unspoken unison their bodies fell to the softness of the thick blue spread. Sam was dimly aware of Greg shrugging out of his shirt, the rest of his clothes closely following to form a forgotten heap beside the pink caftan.

Then he was beside her, his lips beginning an erotic exploration of the seductive valley between her breasts, drinking from the excited peaks that vied for his attention.

Soon . . . hands and mouth were blended into a finely tuned instrument of torture, working with unbelievable precision downward over the nipped-in slimness of her waist, the gentle curve of her hips, and the tender softness of her inner thighs.

Sam clenched her hands in the thickness of Greg's dark hair, writhing beneath him in unconscious abandon.

"Greg . . ." she whispered, urging the hard strength of his body over hers.

"I know, sweetheart . . . I know." His rasping voice sounded in her ear as he settled his weight along the slender length of her.

He entered her quickly, and Sam gasped at the shock of pleasure. With each rhythmic thrust she felt herself being lifted higher and higher, her mind, her thoughts . . . her entire being focused on the center of desire building to a crescendo within her.

Greg held her firmly in his arms as the tide of their lovemaking swept over their glistening bodies, tossing into the swirling whirlpool of oblivion that precedes that final moment of release.

Suddenly the ragged gasp of her name being torn from Greg's lips mingled with Sam's own incoherent cry of fulfillment. They clung together, succumbing to that last heart-stopping surge that tore at them, their hunger sated, their bodies replete.

When at last the world stopped spinning and her mind was slowly awakening from her passionate stupor, Sam felt the heavy weight of Greg's body pressing her further into the softness of the mattress. His dark head was cradled in the curve of her neck . . . his lips touching her skin. One arm was beneath her shoulders, the other tucked against her ribcage, his palm cupping her breast.

Sam smiled drowsily at this unconscious binding of her to him . . . Even in the throes of utmost passion he'd claimed more than her body, possessing her totally and completely and refusing to relinquish his hold over her.

"And why are you grinning like a Cheshire cat?" Greg asked lazily, his hand gently squeezing the creamy mound that boldly nestled beneath his touch. With a motion reminiscent of the lithe sleekness of a huge tiger, he raised his upper body and stared down at her. "I never in my wildest dreams could have imagined it being better between us . . . but it was."

"I know, I felt it too," Sam confessed shakily.

"So when are we going to take proper steps to insure that this happens nightly, daily . . . even in the mornings?" There was a curious alertness about him as he waited for her reply.

"You're insatiable," Sam teased. "Besides, why is it so important that we rush into this contractual agreement you seem so anxious for?"

She wanted him . . . wanted the constancy of a life with him . . . wanted the assurance of his love. But not out of a sense of obligation on his part. There was no reason for some sort of sacrificial atonement for the wrong he'd done her.

"Hell, yes, I'm anxious," he told her after a slight pause. "I haven't forgotten how quickly you can disappear, young lady. So I'll rephrase my question. Can you be ready in two days?"

"That's im—"

"A day?"

"Greg! Stop it!" she squealed in protest. "Have

175

you forgotten that I have a daughter? That I have to make some arrangements for someone to look after her?" She forced back the breathless sensation that was threatening to overwhelm her, and tried at the same time to instill some trace of common sense into his rash timetable.

"Correction, Samantha. *We* have a daughter . . . and, no, I haven't forgotten her. Claire and Jacques . . . along with Sean have agreed to take charge of Elizabeth for a few days."

"I see." She was slightly peeved that he'd discussed their relationship with others, not to mention his arrogant assumption that she would comply so easily. "Don't you think it would have been considerate of you to inform me of your plans before making them public?"

"No, Samantha, I don't." He bent and kissed the pouting curve of her mouth, chuckling at her outrage. "You'd have done the same thing you're doing now, and our wedding would be somewhere in the far-distant future . . . *if* we were lucky," he ruefully remarked. "This way, the decision is out of your hands. I'll be generous and allow you three days."

"You're still bossy and overbearing," she persisted doggedly. "And, for your information, I'm not sure I want Elizabeth staying with Jacques."

Greg shook his head and sighed at her obstinacy. He slid backward and rested his shoulders against the headboard of the bed, hauling a scowling Sam onto his lap. "Isn't it about time you and your brother put an end to this feud?" he suggested patiently, his mouth crinkling at the memory of their past exploits.

"I refuse to bargain with that twerp," she argued, "Jacques left no room for doubt about the way he felt when our marriage broke up."

"Aren't you being just a wee bit hard on him, baby? He was really concerned about you when John died . . . and later, when you had such a difficult time giving birth to Elizabeth. He wasn't content until he had you back in New Orleans."

"That's utter nonsense!" Sam exclaimed. "I made the decision to come back here, and it had nothing to do with my brother."

"Oh?" Greg mused, his breath fanning her cheek as he pressed her head against his shoulder. "Exactly what did cause you to return?"

"My love for a tall, dark, and handsome stranger. He haunted my every waking moment, not to mention my dreams." She wiggled her bottom more snugly between his hard thighs.

"Stranger be damned!" Greg growled, rolling her over onto her back and pinning her to the mattress with the weight of his body. "You came back for me." His shrewd gaze held hers in a captive linkage, his hands framing her face.

"Your conceit is incredible," she taunted.

"So is yours," he countered. "You knew in your soul that the news of your arrival would reach my ears with lightning speed. The only thing that held

177

us up as long as it did was my being out of the country for six weeks. Our meeting was inevitable. Admit it."

"Are you complaining?"

"Hell, no! You merely saved me the trouble of flying to Dallas and camping on your doorstep. Besides, being pursued by the one woman in this world I love has been a heady experience."

"That"—she tapped him lightly on his nose with her forefinger—"will cost you, you arrogant brute."

"A price I'll gladly pay," he murmured against a throbbing nipple, his tongue circling the roseate tip in a leisurely way that was causing Sam to squirm wickedly beneath him.

In less time than seemed possible, she felt the unmistakable rise of Greg's desire for her, her own response meeting and matching his as they joined in the primitive ritual of passion as old as man.

The cove was secluded, its expanse of white sand broken only by the brightly colored beach towels placed side by side.

There was a smile of drowsy contentment on Sam's heart-shaped face, her bikini-clad body tanned a honey gold after four days' exposure the tropical sun.

Four days! For four days she had been Mrs. Greg Howland. By the merest peep between heavily fringed lashes, she caught the brilliant gleam of the large solitaire and the smaller circlet of diamonds in the matching band on the fourth finger of her left hand.

The ceremony had taken place in the privacy of a judge's chambers . . . the judge a personal friend of Greg's. Only family, Mrs. Gautier, Libbie and her husband, and Greg's attorney, Robert Ward, were present.

Sam couldn't help smiling as she remembered her brother's obvious relief at the way whole affair had turned out. "Well, Jacques, you can relax," she told him, "I'm no longer a woman of questionable virtue," which had brought a flush of embarrassment to his handsome face. Greg, who happened to be nearby at the time, stepped in and prevented another clash of wills between his wife and brother-in-law.

"Be nice, Samantha, and stop baiting your brother," he'd drawled in an amused voice, drawing her into the protective circle of his arms.

Self-restraint had never tasted so sweet . . . retreat never as enjoyable as she allowed Greg to lead her over to where Libbie and Sean were carrying on a lively conversation.

The reception, hosted by Claire and Jacques, passed like a pleasant blur in Sam's memory—Greg's nearness, the arm that never left the curve of her waist, more potent than the champagne.

The only sobering moment occurred just prior to their leaving, when Greg drew Sam over to one corner of the room, where Robert Ward was waiting.

"Give Robert the information he needs to start adoption proceedings, Samantha," he instructed her.

Sam caught the tiniest note of determination in his voice and smiled. "Are you sure this is what you want?"

"Very sure." His emerald gaze softened as he looked across the room and saw Elizabeth, her small curly head drooping sleepily in Sean's arms. "Very sure."

Their departure and subsequent flight to the very private island off the coast of Florida had been handled by Greg with the same expertise that was so evident in the preparations for their wedding. Sam was still dizzy from the whirlwind of events, unable to grasp the reality of her dreams finally coming true.

Suddenly the intoxicating mist of contentment was shattered by the feeling of water dripping on her spine. Sam yelped in outraged indignation at this shocking awakening. She twisted round, bracing her upper body on the palms of her hands to face her tormentor.

"That was cruel and inhuman," she informed her grinning husband.

Greg dropped to his knees on the towel, his bronzed body bare except for the briefest of black swimming trunks, his shoulders and hair dripping droplets of water on his glaring wife. He reached for the bottle of tanning lotion. "Not true," he remarked laconically, pouring a generous amount of the lotion on one hand, then applying it to Sam's back. "You were miles away from me and I didn't like it," he remarked, to which Sam had no answer.

Instead of arguing, she gave in to the tantalizing magic of his hands as they worked their way downward from her shoulders to the gentle swell of her buttocks, and back again.

On the upward journey she felt the clip of her bikini top being released. "Greg, don't!" she cried. "Someone will see us."

He chuckled. "Not unless those rocks out there have eyes. That's why I chose this very sheltered spot." His lotioned hands slipped beneath her to cup the sun-warmed firmness of her breasts, his thumb scraping across the tip of her nipples. The peaks engorged throbbingly beneath his touch, and Sam gasped at the rising spiral of desire within her.

With infinite ease Greg turned her over onto her back, fitting her body to the solid length of his. With his free hand he released the ribboned ties below each hip that held the minuscule bikini bottom in place, baring the tanned silkiness of her body to his touch.

"Oh, Greg . . ."

Her own hands stroked his back and waist . . . and on downward, disappearing beneath the abbreviated trunks he wore.

As she touched that part of him that filled the aching emptiness of her desires, Sam felt a convulsive shudder that shook his powerful body.

"What's happened to foreplay?" she asked throati-

181

ly against the heated column of his neck. "Just look- ing into your eyes makes me want you so bad I ache."

"I know, baby, I know," Greg rasped against her breasts as he licked and tasted his way to the core of her desire.

Sam caught at his dark hair with fingers that were stiff from one paroxysm after another that were sweeping over her.

"Now, Greg, now," she cried out, arching against the torturous, teasing thrusts of his tongue against the inner softness of her thighs, each lightning flick drawing her deeper and deeper into the swirling vor- tex of flaming arousal that was now burning out of control.

With a murmured acknowledgment of mutual need, Greg lowered himself to her, finding the turgid warmth of her softness with a swiftness that took her breath away.

Together they rode the crest, their bodies inter- twined, their love a banner that had endured the severest test. In unison they cried out in aching re- lease, their bodies glistening with perspiration, their breathing coming in harshly drawn breaths.

In the midst of the solemn aftermath g raised his head from her breasts, his eyes glowi.. ith love. "Oh, my dearest heart," he whispered, worshiping Sam with his gaze. "I can't believe you're back in my arms again. I'll cherish you through eternity, my darling."

"Don't," Sam whispered, touching a finger to his lips. "You'll have me crying."

"From happiness?"

"Oh, yes, darling, from happiness. A happiness and thankfulness I've never known."

"Thank God for that," Greg murmured, closing his eyes. "Thank God," he breathed, his arms holding her tight.

When You Want A Little More Than Romance—

Try A Candlelight Ecstasy!

Desert Hostage

Diane Dunaway

Behind her is England and her first innocent encounter with love. Before her is a mysterious land of forbidding majesty. Kidnapped, swept across the deserts of Araby, Juliette Barclay sees her past vanish in the endless, shifting sands. Desperate and defiant, she seeks escape only to find harrowing danger, to discover her one hope in the arms of her captor, the Shiek of El Abadan. Fearless and proud, he alone can tame her. She alone can possess his soul. Between them lies the secret that will bind her to him forever, a woman possessed, a slave of love.

A DELL BOOK   11963-4   **$3.95**

A woman's place—the parlor, not the concert stage! But radiant Diana Ballantyne, pianist extraordinaire, had one year before she would bow to her father's wishes, return to England and marry. She had given her word, yet the moment she met the brilliant Maestro, Baron Lukas von Korda, her fate was sealed. He touched her soul with music, kissed her lips with fire, filled her with unnameable desire. One minute warm and passionate, the next aloof, he mystified her, tantalized her. She longed for artistic triumph, ached for surrender, her passions ignited by Vienna dreams.

A DELL BOOK   19530-6 $3.50

Vienna Dreams

by JANETTE RADCLIFFE

THE SEEDS OF SINGING
by Kay McGrath

To the primitive tribes of New Guinea, the
seeds of singing are the essence of courage.
To Michael Stanford and Catherine Morgan,
two young explorers on a lost expedition,
they symbolize a passion that defies war,
separation, and time itself. In the unmapped
highlands beyond the jungle, in a world
untouched since the dawn of time, Michael
and Catherine discover a passion men and
women everywhere only dream about, a love
that will outlast everything.

A DELL BOOK   19120-3 $3.95